THREE TO SEE
THE KING

THREE TO SEE
THE KING

MAGNUS MILLS

Picador USA
New York

www.picadorusa.com

Picador® is a U.S. registered trademark and is used by St. Martin's Press under license from Pan Books Limited.

ISBN 0-312-28355-5

First published in Great Britain by Flamingo
An imprint of HarperCollins*Publishers*

First U.S. Edition: December 2001

10 9 8 7 6 5 4 3 2 1

FOR SUE

1

I live in a house built entirely from tin, with four tin walls, a roof of tin, a chimney and door. Entirely from tin.

My house has no windows because there's nothing to see. Oh, there are shutters that can be used to let the light in when required, but they remain closed against the weather for most of the time. It stands in a wild place, my house, high up on the plain. At night it creaks and groans as the wind batters it for hour after hour, in search of a gap to get inside. Even the door has to be bolted top and bottom to stop it from being blown open. I used to worry in case one day I might lose the roof, but so far that hasn't happened and now I'm certain the structure is quite sound. The man who built it made sure of that. I found the house empty a few years ago, and adopted it for my own use. At first sight I knew it had everything I could need: somewhere to eat and drink and sleep without disturbance, protected from the elements by a layer of corrugated metal and nothing more. A very modest dwelling I must say, but it looked clean and tidy so I moved in. For a long while I was quite content here, and remained convinced I would find no better place to be. Then one day a woman arrived at my door and said, 'So this is where you've been hiding.'

2

She was wrong there. I wasn't hiding from anybody. My house of tin was the place I'd chosen to live. It had nothing to do with hiding, yet the way she put it made me sound as though I'd run away.

You may ask: who was this woman? Well, I hardly knew her really. A friend of a friend I suppose you might say. The last person I'd have expected to turn up, if the truth be known, but she seemed keen on a guided tour so I invited her inside. It was the time of year when the stove had to be kept lit all the time, just to maintain some warmth. She gave a little shiver as I closed the door behind her, and then stood staring around with a sort of surprised smile or half-laugh on her face.

'It's practically bare,' she said.

'Yes,' I replied.

'But you can't live like this.'

'Why not?'

'You just can't.'

I think the sparseness of my existence had caught her out. I had no pictures on the walls to brighten them up, nor any other kind of decoration, and I suppose she was taken aback by how basic it all was. I pointed out that there was a pot of fresh coffee on top of the stove, meaning to show her that it wasn't all 'hardship', but I'm afraid she just laughed again and shook her head.

'Looks like we're going to have to get you sorted out,' she announced.

I realized from the amount of stuff she'd brought with her that she intended to stay around for a while. She had a whole trunkful of clothes, and a vanity case, not to mention the washstand and mirror. Fortunately there was lots of space, more than I needed really, so I told her she could use the upper floor.

I expect you thought my house of tin was a single-roomed affair with a bunk bed in one corner and a bucket in the other. Well, as a matter of fact, nothing could be further from the truth. The man who built it wanted more than just a shack to spend the winter in. He wanted two storeys and a stairway, and a sloping roof with gutters and drainpipes for the rainwater. He built it facing west-south-west, head-on to the wind, and sound enough for any storm. It's a proper house, I tell you, not the kind of ramshackle shanty you might find on some distant seashore where they fish in the morning and sleep in the afternoon. No, you wouldn't catch me living in a place like that. Much better to be somewhere that's going to hold together for a few years, which was why I chose a building foursquare and tall, with an upper floor.

I really thought this woman would be pleased to have a bit of room to herself, but when she saw the stairs she just took one look and said, 'They're very steep, aren't they?'

Well, of course they were steep! What else did she expect in a two storey house of tin? Alright, I admit it was quite a struggle getting the trunk and everything hoisted up, but the way she went on you'd have thought the stairs had been made steep deliberately.

This was what I couldn't understand about her. She'd come all this way to see me, even though we'd only met once or possibly twice before, and yet from the moment she arrived she was full of criticism. By the following morning I'd begun to think she didn't like my domestic arrangements at all. I had spent the whole night conscious of her moving around above me. She didn't seem able to settle down, and it turned out that the wind had kept her awake. I didn't ask her about her sleeplessness directly, of course, because it wouldn't have done for her to know I'd heard her every movement. When she came downstairs, however, the first thing she did was complain about the noise the wind made. Here was an obvious difference between the two of us. It has always astounded me that people can object to such things as being dazzled by sunlight, drenched by the rain or, as in this case, being kept awake by the wind. Surely one of the major appeals of living in a tin house is listening to that very sound! Before this woman turned up I had spent many an hour doing little else, day and night. As I said before, the wind never managed to find a gap to get inside. Nonetheless, it searched and whined incessantly beneath the corrugated eaves, producing a tune of infinite variations. There were times when it would bring with it rain, or else great dry sandstorms that rattled across the roof and added to the general din. These chance harmonics I found reassuring, comforting even, but I'm afraid my new guest heard them with different ears.

'What a racket!' she said, opening the door and looking outside. Then, to my surprise, she exclaimed, 'Oh, sweet!'

Apparently she thought it was quite endearing the way

I'd hung out my washing on the line to dry. Personally, I couldn't see what was supposed to be so remarkable about it. After all, clothes will dry in no time in that wind, so it stood to reason to turn it to full use. Besides, I'd already been up and about for a couple of hours waiting for her to surface, so I thought I might as well get some clothes done. The result of my carrying out this simple chore was striking. She seemed instantly to forget about the wind keeping her awake all night, and now every object she laid eyes on was 'sweet'. She even liked the shovel that I kept on a hook on the back of the door! Maybe it was the morning sun that had put a different glint on things, but whatever the reason I must confess I enjoyed this change of tone. Without her noticing I closed the door again (to prevent the sand from getting inside), and we spent an agreeable morning getting her trunk properly unpacked. Now that the initial prickliness was over I was quite glad she'd come. All the same she took some getting used to. Later I came to understand that she was capable of enjoying my company and finding fault both at the same time, but in those first few days I wasn't sure what was going on.

Take the question of the mirror, for example. The one she'd brought with her was a full-length model, and it was still waiting to be moved to the upper floor. I put this job off for a while, then just when I was in the middle of lifting it up she announced it was probably better to leave it where it was.

'Don't worry,' I replied. 'It's not too heavy.'

'So you're taking it up are you?' she asked.

'Yes,' I said. 'Might as well.'

When finally I'd got it to the top of the stairs she came and joined me.

'You've got smears on it now,' she said. 'Look.'

'Couldn't be helped,' I answered.

'You didn't have to bring it up here at all. I'd have much preferred it down by the door. The light's more natural there.'

'Well why didn't you say?'

'I did!' she snapped. 'Thanks very much! Now you've got smears on it!'

When I offered to take the mirror back down she told me not to bother, so I didn't, and another three or four days went by before she mentioned it again. On this second occasion she pointed out exactly where she wanted it, rather than suggesting what was 'probably better' or what was 'preferable'. I obliged by moving the mirror with good grace, taking care not to get any more smears on it. In this way we managed between us to smooth relations over, and most of the time we seemed to get on quite well together.

Even so, I couldn't work out what exactly she'd come for. I mean, there was nothing to keep her in my house of tin. She was very welcome to stay as long as she liked, of course, but I'd have thought she'd be better off living somewhere where there were more people, instead of here amongst a few scattered individuals on a wild and blustery plain.

Each night I heard her moving restlessly around on the upper floor, disturbed by those very elements that for years had been lulling me to sleep. The trouble was, now I couldn't sleep either. Every time the building creaked and groaned in the autumn gales I felt a wave of guilt, as though it was me personally who was keeping her awake. Still, I tried to make the best of it. Each morning I rose early, took the shovel and cleared away the drifts of red sand that were beginning to gather on the windward side of the house. At least this would save her from being blocked in if she decided to leave. As the weather continued to deteriorate, however, this seemed increasingly unlikely. Having established herself on the upper floor she now started to make incursions into the area around the stove. Anyone with a house of tin will tell you that, given a good coal supply, the stove is always regarded as the engine room. The heat needed for cooking, washing and generally keeping warm makes it the natural centre of operations, and this woman grasped the fact very quickly. Within a week the seat by the stove had become hers, whether she occupied it or not. Needless to say I was allowed to use it in between times, but only in the sense that I was borrowing it from her. This was fine by me because mostly I was engaged with tasks that kept me on my feet. I'd decided to check the outside of the house to make sure none of the creaks and groans were due to structural weakness. I'm pleased to say they weren't, and that the sounds we heard in the night were mostly those of expansion and contraction.

The mirror, in the meantime, had gone through a trial period in the place she'd suggested near the doorway. This had proved satisfactory, so one afternoon I gave it a permanent fixing, which seemed to please her. On the rare days that the weather was mild and still, she would stand with the door open examining her reflection full-length in the natural light. I have to admit to being fairly impressed by the trouble she went to over her appearance, considering there was no one else present apart from myself. Once or twice she would catch me watching as she made adjustments to her waist or hemline, at which point she'd give me a very pleasant smile.

The trunk on the upper floor seemed to contain an endless hoard of clothing, which she never tired of trying on in various combinations. This was in direct contrast to my own wardrobe. I had two sets of clothes which I alternated when they got dirty, and that was that. Fortunately, she didn't ever go on about my choice of attire. In many respects she was content for me to continue my life just as it had been before she arrived, without any interference. Which was fair enough when you think about it. She was only a guest, after all, and there was a limit to what she could or could not influence. Indeed, I'd even started to notice that the bouts of criticism were becoming rarer. We passed the time fully aware of one another's presence, and went to every effort to avoid friction when possible.

Then one day she said, out of the blue, 'So what became of your great plan?'

'What great plan?' I replied.

'You told me you were going to live in a canyon.'

'Oh that,' I said. 'Well, it never quite came to fruition.'

'But how can it have never come to fruition?' she asked, 'when you had such hopes and aspirations? You told me all about them. One day, you said, you were going to make a voyage, the culmination of which would be your discovery of a canyon, deep and wide, and cut through the reddest of earth. Then, when you'd surveyed it from end to end and found the perfect site, you were going to build a house entirely from tin.'

It turned out she was referring to some conversation we'd had when we last met. I remembered none of it, but apparently she could recall in detail almost every word I'd said. As a matter of fact, she seemed to know quite a lot about me, about my tastes, about my interests, and even about my future plans. I soon began to wonder exactly how much information she'd managed to glean from that one exchange. For my part, all I knew about her was her name.

3

As she reminded me of my scheme in all its detail, I pondered on how I could have come to abandon it so easily. What had distracted and led me on such a different path? The answer, I soon realized, lay in the moment I'd stumbled upon my present abode. With one look I had allowed myself to be seduced by its grace and solidity, by its warm stove, and by its shutters that could be closed against the weather. Oh yes, it was a house of tin alright, but instead of being in a canyon, it was situated high up on the plain!

I opened the door and gazed out across that vast expanse, asking myself if I'd left it too late to resume my search. It was the afternoon of a desolate winter's day, and as I stood there a savage gust of wind warned of the hardship that such a life would bring. Quickly, I stepped back into the warmth.

'There probably isn't even a canyon,' I said, by way of explanation.

'How far did you look?' she asked.

'Quite far.'

'And you found nothing?'

'No.'

'Well, I suppose it hardly matters really,' she remarked. 'As long as you've got a roof over your head.'

Maybe so, but I was curious as to why she'd raised the subject in the first place. At no time had she questioned my desire to live in a canyon, and seemed only concerned with my obvious failure to do so. At first I assumed this was simply another criticism to add to the current list. After a while, however, I began to suspect there was more to it than that. Nothing else was said about my unfulfilled plans, nor did she mention them again over the next few days. Instead, she adopted a strategy of silence, during which I couldn't help thinking that she was waiting for me to do something. Over and over again I felt her eyes on me as I carried out some domestic duty in the house. When I brought some extra pillows to the upper floor, for example, she sat on her bed watching while I struggled to get them into their covers. She didn't utter a single word, but instead looked at me as if to say, 'You're wasting your time doing that: there are much more important things to be getting on with.'

This unsatisfactory state of affairs continued for almost a week, and at last I could stand it no longer.

'Right,' I said, one cold, bright morning. 'I'm going out.'

'Where?' she asked.

'To look for a canyon to live in. I might be gone a while.'

'But I don't want to be here on my own,' she protested.

'Don't you?'

'Of course not.'

'Very well,' I said. 'I'll sort that out first.'

I put my boots on and went over to see a neighbour of mine called Simon Painter. He lived a couple of miles away to the west, in a tin house of similar construction to my own. This Simon Painter moved into the vicinity round about the same time as me, and I suppose you could call him a friend. To tell the truth, though, 'half-friend half-nuisance' would be a much better description. The trouble with Simon was that he tried too hard to be sociable, frequently turning up at odd hours of the day on so-called surprise visits which generally involved exchanging unnecessary gifts. These calls were fine so long as they were also short-lived, but unfortunately he had a tendency to outstay his welcome and often needed to be shown the door. For limited periods, however, he was a good companion, and for this reason I knew he could be relied on for what I had in mind.

I should mention that Simon Painter was not my only neighbour, but he was by far the nearest. Living beyond him were Steve Treacle and Philip Sibling, and strewn around the area were two or three others whom I'd never met, all separated by intervals of several miles. The only thing we had in common was that we each lived alone in a house built from tin. We rarely saw one another because we preferred it like that. So went my understanding of the arrangement anyway.

The last time I'd laid eyes on Simon was when he came over to tell me he was planning to hoist a captive balloon above his house. Did I have any objections, he wanted to know. Well obviously I didn't, and I realized he'd made the journey simply as an excuse to visit somebody. I had no doubt that he'd also called upon each of the others under the same pretext. The idea of this balloon, apparently, was to make his residence more easily identifiable. I knew for a fact that it was already equipped with a flagpole on the roof and a bell that chimed whenever the wind blew. This proposed new addition confirmed an opinion I'd held for some time, namely, that Simon Painter was trying to attract attention to himself. Why he'd chosen to live in such a remote setting I couldn't understand, because he seemed to spend his days seeking the fellowship of other people. I'd lost count of the many occasions (when the wind was in the right direction) that I'd heard his bell clanging forlornly in the dead of night. If I could hear it at such a distance, then surely it must have kept him wide awake, which seemed a high price to pay.

Of course, it wouldn't have done to question Simon's presence on this wide and deserted plain. He always swore that it was the place where he'd found contentment, and he would have denied any suggestion to the contrary. Nevertheless, I wasn't entirely convinced.

As I approached his house the first thing I saw was the balloon anchored above it. Large enough, at a guess, to support the weight of two or three men, this balloon swayed gently at the end of a long rope. Next I saw his flag, brightly coloured in a combination of orange and purple, flapping at the top of its pole, and indicating that Simon Painter was 'at home'.

Drawing nearer to his house of tin, it was odd to think that I wasn't the only person to occupy such a dwelling. Recently I'd spent so much time in or around my own place that I'd come to believe I was unique; that there was no one else in the world with such an interesting existence. My visit to Simon Painter reminded me that there were, in fact, several of us. His walls and roof gave off a dull gleam in the morning sunlight, and for a few moments I could only stand and stare at such a perfect spectacle.

The clanging of Simon's bell interrupted my reverie. A breeze was getting up, but I noticed the shutters on the house were all wide open, which must have created quite a draught. Then I heard a joyful cry from within. This told me there would be no need to knock.

'Oh hello!' called Simon as he threw open the door. 'Come in! Come in! This is a pleasant surprise!'

I knew for a fact that he would have been watching through the shutters from the moment I appeared in the distance, but I said nothing as I had no wish to contradict him. He held the door open with one hand, and shook mine with the other. At the same time I remembered a feature of his house that I could never quite understand. For some reason he had the door opening outwards, which seemed to me a most inconvenient arrangement. It meant he had to reach right round the outside to close it whenever it was hooked open, or else there was a risk of it slamming shut when it wasn't. Much better, surely, to have the door swinging into the house. Then it could be open and closed with ease, and the flow of air regulated as required. Simon's insistence on having an outward-opening door only served to substantiate my judgement that he just wanted to be different from everyone else. To be fair on him, though, he was always a most genial host. As soon as we were inside he had me sitting at the table with a cup of coffee in front of me.

'Well, well,' he kept saying. 'Lovely to see you. Lovely to see you!'

As a gift for Simon I'd brought along a set of wind chimes, and I now presented them to him formally.

'You could hang them up beside your bell,' I suggested. 'To keep it company.'

'Thank you,' he replied. 'Yes, excellent idea.'

'Speaking of which,' I continued. 'Did you know I had a guest?'

'At your house of tin?' he asked.

'Yes,' I replied. 'Of course.'

'Sorry for asking, but . . . it's just that I rarely have visitors here . . . and . . . well . . . who is it?'

'This woman I know.'

'A woman?' Instantly he sprang to his feet, went to the nearest shutter and looked out. 'Is she there now?'

'Yes,' I said. 'But you can't see her from here.'

'Well, you must bring her over!'

'Why don't you come to mine instead? You can keep her company.'

'Alright, I will, yes.'

He had a bag packed within minutes. Then he closed down the stove so that it would go out of its own accord, fastened down all the shutters and lowered his flag. Soon after that we were on our way back to my house. Most of the journey he didn't speak at all, which was unlike him, but as we got nearer he finally broke his silence.

'By the way,' he asked. 'What's your guest's name?'

'Mary Petrie,' I said. 'Do you know her?'

'No, no,' he replied. 'I don't know any women.'

The instant we went through the door I remembered I hadn't told her I was bringing someone back with me. She was standing at the top of the stairs, looking down on us.

'This is Simon Painter,' I explained. 'The person I went to see this morning.'

'He's got an overnight bag,' she replied.

'Yes, he's come to stay for a while.'

'Pleased to meet you,' said Simon.

'Pleased to meet you,' she answered, without looking at him.

At this moment Simon displayed a flair for diplomacy which I didn't know he had, and stepped outside again.

'Oh marvellous view!' we could hear him saying. 'Absolutely marvellous.'

I advanced halfway up the stairs towards Mary Petrie.

'What's he doing here?' she asked.

'He's come to keep you company.'

'What for?'

'You said you didn't want to be here on your own.'

'That wasn't what I meant.'

'Wasn't it?'

'Of course not.'

'Well, what did you mean then?'

She looked at me for a long time. The expression on her face did not change, but at last I understood.

4

I tell you, I was up those stairs in two strides! For the next half minute or so I forgot about the sublime and esoteric pleasures of living in a house of tin! I forgot about the wind that blasts across the plain all night and day. And I forgot about Simon Painter, waiting at a discreet distance outside the door.

Mary Petrie, however, had not forgotten him.

'That'll do for now,' she murmured in my ear. 'You'll just have to wait until he's gone.'

'OK,' I said. 'I'll get rid of him.'

This was easier said than done. When I got downstairs and saw Simon standing there with his overnight bag, I knew I couldn't just turn him away.

'Everything alright?' he asked.

'Yes,' I replied. 'Fine.'

'I'm not in the way then?'

'No, of course not.'

'Thanks,' he said, smiling. 'House is looking good.'

'Yes, I try to keep it ship-shape.' I laid my hand on the

tin wall and noticed how cold it felt. 'Why don't you come in?'

Mary Petrie' was still standing at the top of the stairs, looking down at us, when we entered. I sat Simon at the table then quickly went back up to her.

'He'll have to stay a while,' I said, lowering my voice. 'He came here especially.'

'That's up to you,' she answered. 'I've got plenty of time.'

Her voice was the softest I'd ever heard it. She came down to meet our guest properly, and he rose to meet her.

'So you're Simon Painter,' she said. 'How nice to put a face to a name.'

As a matter of fact I'd never mentioned him before, but he seemed so pleased with the remark that I didn't say anything. During the following hours she treated him to all her charms, and made him feel thoroughly at home. Meanwhile, I kept wondering how long we could expect him to stay. In truth, I had only one thing on my mind at that moment, and there was definitely no part in it for Simon Painter. I also asked myself why she'd left it so long to let her feelings be revealed. To think she'd been staying here all that time and I'd had no idea! A few words would have been enough to let me know, but instead she'd kept it all to herself. Now, as I watched her entertaining Simon so generously, she appeared in no particular hurry to get shot of him. The events of the afternoon had held great promise, yet it was almost as if she was taking delight in further prolonging the outcome. From time to time she glanced at me with sparkling eyes and smiled. Mostly, though, her attention was turned to Simon.

As for him, he was basking in every moment. He talked and talked about how wonderful it was for the three of us to be sitting together like this, enjoying each other's companionship with the stove to keep us warm. It tran-spired that in the few minutes it had taken him to pack he'd managed to include a gift. This was a framed picture of his house of tin, which Mary Petrie accepted with good grace and placed on the shelf.

'Very kind of you,' she said.

'My pleasure,' he replied. 'It's traditional in these parts to come bearing gifts.'

Well it was the first I'd heard of it! I had taken Simon a present that morning because I knew he expected one, and for no other reason whatsoever. The way he spoke about it being 'traditional in these parts' made it sound as though everyone in the locality was part of some big happy family. The reality, of course, was quite different. As far as I knew nobody saw anyone else from one month to the next because they all wanted to be independent. The idea of being regarded as one of the 'folk' who lived in tin houses and who came bearing gifts made me feel quite uneasy. Yet one look at Simon told me he believed he was stating a fact.

The picture itself, of course, couldn't have been less inter-esting. After all, who wants a view of someone else's home? There was hardly any difference between Simon's dwelling and mine but, nevertheless, the picture remained on display for the entire duration of his visit.

This turned out to be almost a week. Mary Petrie made him feel so welcome that it would have been difficult for him to leave any sooner. At the end of the first evening she smiled at us both before saying goodnight and heading up the stairs. Hours later I realized she was no longer moving around restlessly above me. Instead, I was being kept awake by Simon talking in his sleep. The corrugated walls creaked and groaned as they sheltered us from the steadily rising wind. A few days more and I would be alone with Mary Petrie. For the time being, however, my house of tin had three residents.

In the morning I overslept. When finally I awoke the first thing I heard was Simon clumping around on the roof. Mary Petrie had risen before me and stood tending the stove.

'How come you're up so early?' I asked.

'I thought I'd make the pair of you some coffee.'

'Thanks,' I said. 'What's he doing up there?'

'He's seeing if there's anywhere to put a flagpole.'

'I don't want a flagpole!'

'He seems to think you do.'

'Well, I don't!'

I got up and went outside just as Simon came clambering down.

'I hope you haven't left any dents,' I said. 'That roof's not for walking about on.'

'No, no, I've been quite careful,' he replied. 'Did you know you can see my house from up there?'

'The balloon or the house itself?' I asked.

'Both,' he said.

'No, I didn't.'

This was the sort of news I'd rather not have heard. As far as I was concerned, Simon Painter's house and those of my other neighbours were positioned somewhere beyond the horizon. I found it quite disconcerting to think that, after all, we might each live within sight of one another, even if it was only from the roof. For a long time I'd been convinced that I occupied a remote and unusual part of the world. Suddenly I wasn't so sure.

'You could fix a flagpole up there no trouble if you wanted,' declared Simon.

'Well, thanks for having a look,' I replied. 'But I don't really want one.'

'I've a spare pole back at home.'

'No, it's alright.'

'Well, if you ever do put one up, don't forget I've got plenty of flags.'

'I'll bear it in mind.'

Prior to going back inside I intended to clear away the sand that had drifted against the walls overnight. I quite liked doing this first thing in the morning as it gave me a bit of an appetite before breakfast, but when I got hold of the shovel I realized the job had already been done. The loose sand was all lying beyond the ends of the house where it could blow away freely. It had been moved there by Simon.

'You ought to set up some windbreaks,' he said. 'Then you wouldn't have a problem with sand.'

'It's not a problem,' I replied. 'I like clearing it away actually.'

As I stood there with the redundant shovel I noticed Mary Petrie watching through the open doorway.

'Now how are you going to pass the time?' she asked.

'Can you close that door please?' I snapped. 'I don't want sand getting into the house.'

She closed it slowly and deliberately, watching me intently as the crack grew smaller. Mary Petrie, of course, knew better than anyone just how difficult the next few days promised to be. How indeed was I to pass the time until Simon left? Before now I'd seldom been concerned with such questions. Existing in a house of tin was an end unto itself, a particular state of being, and time didn't come into it. You did not need to know what time it was, for example, to witness dry lightning as it flashed across the plain at dusk. Or to feel the threat of an approaching storm. These things occurred independently of time, which was why there was no clock in my house. I simply had no need for one. Nonetheless, as I led Simon back inside for breakfast, I realized that time was already beginning to slow down.

It didn't help that until yesterday he hadn't spoken to anyone for weeks. Silence was clearly not his vocation, and now he was making up the deficit. I'd never come across anyone who talked so much! He could keep going for hours on end without a break! Worse, he seemed to think that a conversation consisted of asking a question, listening to the answer, adding his own comment and then asking another. I would have been quite content to sit peacefully at the table and talk about subjects as and when they cropped up. Every time there was the slightest period of silence, though, Simon felt obliged to interrupt it.

'Heard anything of Steve Treacle lately?' he would begin.

'No, I haven't,' I'd reply.

'Nor me. I went over to his place about a month ago, but he wasn't at home. Well there was no answer when I knocked on the door, anyway. I never seem to be able to catch him these days. Last time was when I was making preliminary enquiries about my captive balloon. Incidentally, I take it you've still no objections to that?'

'No, of course not.'

'That's good. I gather Steve's recently become great friends with Philip Sibling.'

'Really?'

'Yes. Have you seen anything of him?'

'Philip?'

'Yes.'

'No.'

'Nor me.'

And so it would go on. At some point in the exchange Mary Petrie would rise from the table, glance at the two of us, and proceed to the upper floor. I was sure she was enjoying all this in her own way because there always seemed to be a slight smile on her lips as she disappeared from view. Her graceful departure would cause Simon to cease talking for a moment while his gaze followed her movement up the stairs. Then the quietness would get the better of him and he'd be off again.

'Apparently there's someone living even further out than Steve and Philip,' he announced one evening. 'His name's Michael Hawkins. Do you know him?'

'No, sorry,' I replied.

'I'll have to wander out there and see him sometime. Make contact, sort of thing, so he doesn't feel too cut off. Would you be interested in coming along?'

'Probably not, actually.'

'Oh . . . er . . . alright,' said Simon, momentarily silenced.

The suggestion that this Michael Hawkins was 'further out' than the rest of us I found quite irritating. I mean to say, it wasn't as if we were all strung along some wild frontier beyond which no one could live. I had no doubts that Michael Hawkins deliberately chose to be 'cut off' as Simon put it, and that was precisely why he dwelt in such a place. This didn't mean, however, that he was somehow different or more interesting than anybody else. Besides which, who was to say who was further out than the next fellow? I'd have thought it depended on the starting point really. I was tempted to take Simon to task on the matter, but I realized that with his point of view it would be a complete waste of time. Instead, I had a question of my own, just for a change.

'Do you know if this Michael Hawkins lives in a house made entirely from tin?' I asked.

'Yes, so I understand.'

'And how long has he been there?'

'Quite long.'

'Longer than I've been here?'

'I believe so, yes.'

'Well,' I remarked. 'If he thinks he's established some kind of outpost then he's a fool.'

At these words Simon gave me a very puzzled look before quickly changing the subject.

That night I did not sleep well. There was a gale blowing outside, and I kept having this tangled up dream involving me, Mary Petrie and Michael Hawkins, in which he was in my bed and she wasn't. Several times I woke up wondering where she'd gone, and not until the morning did it occur to me that she hadn't been there in the first place. Furthermore, the person I'd thought was Michael Hawkins turned out to be Simon, fast asleep in the spare bed a few feet away. Considering I'd never even met Michael Hawkins I found this dream quite disturbing. It was almost as if I was suddenly in a competition against him, yet why this should be so I couldn't imagine. I decided to forget all about it, so at first light I got up and went out to clear away the overnight sand. A large pile had accumulated on the windward side of the house, but after an hour's work with the shovel I had it reduced to manageable proportions. The gale had subsided into a strong breeze. It was coming from the west, and now and again I heard the faint notes of Simon's bell clanging in the distance. All across the plain I could see red sand on the move, drifting in tiny particles. This was the roughest time of year to be in a place like this. I looked at my house of tin, knowing it would be some while before I saw it glinting in the sunlight once more. The sky had turned grey, and I was sure I could expect more gales in the next few weeks. My thoughts turned to Simon's suggestion about setting up some windbreaks. Come to think of it, this wasn't a bad idea at all, and I began to wonder if I should give it serious consideration.

Then the door opened and Mary Petrie emerged.

'You're being very patient,' she said.

'Yes,' I replied. 'Suppose I am.'

'Not that you've got any choice, of course.'

'No.'

'Still,' she observed. 'You seem happy enough out here with your little shovel.'

'Do I?'

'Yes, quite sweet really.' She picked up a handful of sand, allowing the grains to slip gradually through her fingers. 'Who's this Michael Hawkins?'

'How do you know about him?' I asked.

'I heard the pair of you talking last night.'

'Well you know as much as I do then.'

'Aren't you curious to meet him?'

'Why should I be?'

'Well, he's a neighbour, isn't he?'

'Not really,' I said. 'He lives miles away.'

Mary Petrie moved nearer and lowered her voice. 'Simon's going to see him.'

'Is he?'

'Yes, he's just told me.'

'When?'

'Today,' she said. 'He's packing his bag at this very moment.'

'Well, why didn't you tell me before?'

Instantly I dropped the shovel and went into the house.

There was Simon, all wrapped up in his coat and ready to leave.

'Morning,' I said, giving him my best smile. 'You off then?'

'Yes,' he replied. 'I've been thinking about this Michael Hawkins and I really feel I ought to go and say hello to him.'

'You're probably right.'

'So I'll get moving this morning if that's OK with you.'

'Of course,' I said. 'Don't forget to take him a gift.'

'Oh, thanks for reminding me. I'll drop in at my place on the way and find something suitable.'

He picked up his bag and headed for the door.

Then Mary Petrie said, 'You'd better have some breakfast before you go.'

5

I was really beginning to think she was doing it on purpose.
I mean to say, Simon was just about to walk through the
door when she said this! Next minute he'd taken his coat
off again and was sitting down at the table. By now, of
course, I'd worked up quite an appetite of my own, so I
found myself in a very weak position. Then I realized that
the best course of action was to play her at her own game.
I was the host and therefore I had to do the cooking, but I
certainly wasn't going to make her anything. Instead I gave
Simon the best breakfast he'd ever had.

'Marvellous,' he said, when I placed it before him.
'You're so kind.'

Mary Petrie, in the meantime, retired to the upper floor
without saying another word. I could hear her moving
around up there, humming softly to herself. It sounded as
if she was putting fresh covers on the bed. As I looked at
the coffee pot heating over the stove, and listened to the
sand chafing against the tin walls, the inside of my house
suddenly felt very warm and comfortable. It wasn't really
a day for a person to be setting off to see someone he'd

never met before, especially when he wasn't even expected, and it occurred to me that Simon could very easily change his mind about going. He certainly looked contented enough, sitting there at the table.

After about an hour, however, he stretched himself and said, 'Well, I think I'll be getting along now.'

'You sure you've had enough?' I asked.

'Quite sure, thanks,' he replied, rising from his chair.

After he'd got his bag he hovered awkwardly for a moment at the foot of the stairs.

'Bye then Mary!' he called.

'Bye Simon,' we heard her say. 'Have a nice journey.'

A minute later I said goodbye to him and closed the door. At last we had the place to ourselves.

*   *   *

I won't go into any of the details of what happened next, but needless to say my period of exile from the upper floor came to an end there and then. We passed the next three or four days shut inside the house, never even bothering to look outside. Here, I thought, was true fulfilment. With Mary Petrie lying in my bed I knew I had everything a man could need: somewhere to eat and drink and sleep without disturbance, and a good woman. We were warm and snug in a paradise made from tin! Then, just as I was about to drift into a state of permanent hibernation, the honeymoon suddenly ended.

It happened when I remembered I hadn't been out to clear away the sand for some time. I went downstairs and opened the door, to be confronted with a great pile that practically fell inside. Closing the door again I sat and got my boots on, just as Mary Petrie joined me. She took her usual place next to the stove.

'If this had been Simon Painter's house we'd have been in trouble,' I remarked. 'His door opens outwards so we'd be blocked in.'

'That's alright,' she said, smiling. 'We'd just have to wait till we were rescued.'

'It's a serious matter actually,' I replied.

Taking the broom I began sweeping up the remnants of sand that had spilled through the doorway.

'Stop that at once!' cried Mary Petrie.

I looked at her and noticed the smile had disappeared.

'What's the matter?'

'I don't want you doing that while I'm here,' she said. 'The sand goes everywhere.'

'That's why I'm sweeping it up,' I said.

'Not when I'm here!' she exclaimed.

'When then?'

'When I go out! Look, I'll be going for a walk later. Do it then.'

'Alright, but I didn't know you'd be going out, did I?'

'Well, you know now.'

Feeling slightly shell-shocked by this sudden burst of hostility I went outside and shovelled away the drift, taking care to keep well clear of the door. All morning I kept at it, before and after breakfast, working in a wind that showed no sign of letting up. The weather had turned quite cold now, and I wondered if Mary Petrie was serious about going for a walk. Sure enough, though, sometime around noon she came out of the house wearing a big coat, and set off without saying anything. I watched as her diminishing figure headed into the distance. Then, when she was reduced to a tiny speck on the horizon, she turned and began to follow a wide arc around the house. This was the time I was supposed to be sweeping up inside, so I quickly went and got on with it. When I'd finished there wasn't a grain of sand anywhere, and the whole place was looking spick-and-span. Expecting Mary Petrie to be back at any time I prepared some coffee, then went to the doorway and looked out. At first I couldn't see her at all, but as my eyes became accustomed to the daylight I spotted her far away to the west. I then realized she was walking a full circle, keeping the house just in sight. It dawned on me at the same moment that this was the first occasion I'd been there on my own for quite a while, so I decided to make the most of it. I went back inside, closed the door, and resumed my former pastime of listening to the walls creak in the blustery wind. When she returned about an hour later, I was on the verge of dozing into a peaceful sleep.

'I could hear a bell clanging somewhere out there,' she said, as she removed her coat.

'It's Simon Painter's,' I explained. 'To let people know where he lives. Have a good walk, did you?'

'Yes, thanks. Quite invigorating.'

'Is that why you went out?' I asked. 'To be invigorated?'

'Not really, no,' she answered.

It wasn't until the next day that I discovered the true reason. I'd got up fairly early and been out to clear away yet more sand. By the time Mary Petrie came down I was sitting at the table having breakfast.

'Quite windy again last night,' I said.

'Yes,' she replied. 'I heard it.'

'I expect Simon Painter's door'll be blocked up.'

She sighed, but said nothing.

'He really ought to have it opening inwardly,' I continued. 'That'd be a much better arrangement by far.'

'Right,' she said, reaching for her coat. 'I'm going out.'

'Already?' I asked. 'You've only just got up.'

'I don't care. I'm not staying cooped up here with you all day.'

'Why, what have I done?'

'You keep going on about Simon's house.'

'No, I don't.'

'Yes you do. You're always criticizing it.'

'Well,' I said. 'I only mentioned his door opened the wrong way.'

'There you go again,' she said. 'I'm not interested.'

'But you must be interested. You live in a house of tin yourself.'

'Look!' she snapped. 'I'm going out! See you later.'

From then on she went for a walk every day, sometimes saying goodbye and sometimes not. After she'd gone I'd quickly do any sweeping up that was needed, before settling down to enjoy the brief period I had the place to myself.

On these occasions I would sit and think about what had happened to me. It was quite remarkable really. One day I'd been living alone in a house of tin, minding my own business. Then suddenly this woman, this Mary Petrie, had moved in, and everything had changed. Now I was subject to rules, such as where I could sit and when I should sweep up, and there were matters I was not allowed to discuss, or at least go on about too much. As I waited for her return it also struck me how swiftly I'd adapted to my new situation.

To be fair I suppose Mary Petrie had adapted too, in her own way. She was the last person I would have expected to live in a house of tin in the middle of a vast and deserted plain, but I had to admit she was trying to make the best of it. Those long walks, for example, soon became an important part of her day. She always began by heading for a point in the distance, and then she would turn and follow an encircling course right around the house. She varied it by going clockwise or anti-clockwise, but she made sure she never went completely out of sight. Her starting point in the circle seemed to be chosen at random, and each time she set off I would look with interest to see whether she first went north, west, east, or south. Sometimes, when I was watching her move along in the distance, I would see her stop and then appear to be examining the ground. On these occasions she would return and show me a stone she'd found whose shape she thought interesting. Or maybe an unusual glass bottle. Generally she'd be in a better mood when she got back than when she went out, but she'd also be quite cold, so I always made sure the stove was fired up in readiness.

The walks weren't the only way she adjusted to her new life. Before long there was a vase on the table containing an arrangement of dry grasses she'd collected. Meanwhile, the upper walls were hung with pictures, each depicting a dancer standing in a different pose.

She had plans for the shutters too.

'We'll have them open in the spring,' she announced one breezy afternoon. 'Once all this sand has stopped flying about.'

I knew, though, that spring would be a long time coming. She hadn't spent a whole winter here before, and had no real idea how long it might last. There wasn't likely to be much rain or snow, I was quite sure of that, but we could expect several more weeks of high winds yet. From my own point of view it didn't make any difference if it was winter, spring, summer or autumn: all of them were equally interesting to someone used to dwelling in a house of tin. On the other hand, when I saw Mary Petrie being buffeted daily by the gales, I wondered just how long her endurance would last.

I also feared she might get bored after a while. She changed her clothes several times a day, and told me it was so that she'd have suitable attire for whatever she happened to be doing. Privately, though, I suspected she was attempting to break each day into shorter spans.

Another sign of boredom was when she amused herself by teasing me. Usually I wouldn't have minded this, as I can take a joke same as the next man. Unfortunately, she often chose to raise the subject of my failed plan for living in a canyon. She seemed to have grasped that this was quite a sensitive matter with me, but instead of avoiding it she brought it up in conversations all the time.

One day, for example, she said, 'You know that canyon you wanted to live in?'

'Yes,' I replied. 'What about it?'

'Would there be a river in the bottom?'

'Could be.'

'Cos if there was you'd need a canoe, wouldn't you?'

'Suppose so, yes.'

'But you haven't got a paddle.'

'No.'

'So you'd be up a creek without a paddle!'

She then dissolved into a fit of giggling, while I was supposed to sit there and smile politely. As I said before, I can take a joke the same as the next man, but I didn't really like it when she kept reminding me about that canyon. To avoid the situation I tried to think of ways to stop her from getting bored, and the solution I came up with was to offer to accompany her on her walks. We tried this once, only to discover that we both went at completely different speeds. I ended up arriving home about half an hour before her, so we decided not to bother again.

'Besides,' she pointed out. 'The whole idea of the walks is for me to get away from you for a bit.'

*   *   *

Early one morning I became aware of a gentle drumming noise. I was lying in bed, half asleep, listening to the gale outside and wondering how much sand had accumulated overnight. At first I didn't notice the noise at all, as it almost blended in with the more familiar renderings produced by the house.

Almost, that is, but not quite.

The difference about this drumming was its highly rhythmical quality, so unlike the normal desultory attacks made by the elements. As if to demonstrate the point, a particularly severe blast of wind struck against the walls and brought me fully awake. When it faded away I realized that the drumming had changed. Now, all of a sudden, the rhythm had sped up. Then it stopped altogether.

At this moment Mary Petrie stirred a little, so that the sheets and blankets rustled. By the time she'd settled down again the drumming had resumed. It was coming, as far as I could tell, from downstairs. I began to suspect that maybe an empty kettle or pan had been left on top of the stove, and was expanding as it heated up. But, surely, if it had been there all night the bottom would have melted by now, wouldn't it? Anyway, this noise wasn't really sharp enough for that. It was altogether softer and duller. I listened for another full minute and during that time the rhythm changed twice again.

Then Mary Petrie awoke and said, 'Is it raining?'

'No,' I replied.

'What's that drumming noise then?'

'Don't know.'

'Well, aren't you going to go and find out?'

'Could do I suppose, but I'm quite comfortable here.'

A few more seconds passed. The drumming persisted.

'Go on,' she urged. 'After all, it could be a serious matter.'

Reluctantly, I rolled out of bed and put some clothes on, then headed for the stairs. It wasn't until I was halfway down that a thought occurred to me. Hadn't I heard this sound somewhere before? I stopped and listened again. It had now become much more emphatic than it was earlier, and my suspicion increased. Moving more quietly I continued to make my way downstairs. With utmost stealth I slid aside the bolts at the top and bottom of the door. Then, very slowly, I opened it by about two inches. Through the crack I saw Steve Treacle, crouched down at the corner of the house, drumming on the wall with his knuckles. He was concentrating very hard on this activity, with his face close down by his hand, and didn't notice me. I opened the door a little further. Standing about fifteen feet away, his collar turned against the wind, was Philip Sibling. He was watching Steve's antics with a tired expression on his face. I managed to catch his eye, and he shook his head in a resigned manner. I put my finger to my lips. He nodded. I closed the door. Treading very lightly, I went to the point on the inside wall that corresponded with Steve's position.

I allowed him a few more seconds of drumming, then suddenly banged hard on the wall with a hammer.

There was a startled cry.

6

Pulling my boots on, I went outside to greet my guests formally. Steve was now standing about six feet from the house with a surprised look on his face.

'Made you jump, did I?' I asked.

'Yes,' he replied.

'Well, why can't you just knock on the door like normal people?'

'I was trying to wake you gradually, by degrees.'

'It's a tried and tested technique,' added Philip.

Each of them was wearing an identical heavy coat, but all the same I could see they were both quite chilly.

'I've got a good mind not to invite you in,' I remarked. 'Now don't forget to wipe your feet.'

'Is that the latest rule then?' asked Steve.

'Yes,' I said. 'There's a whole new regime here.'

I hadn't seen either Steve or Philip for quite a while, and it was good to renew the acquaintanceship. What seemed surprising, though, was the fact of their turning up together. I vaguely recalled Simon Painter mentioning that they'd become friends, but to tell the truth I'd thought this was just wishful thinking, as it fitted perfectly into his scheme for everybody to be friendly with everyone else. The thing I least expected was a joint visit from two individuals I regarded very much as 'loners'.

Besides, it had always struck me that Steve was the sort of person who'd tax anyone's patience after a while. He had his own way of doing everything, even down to announcing his arrival at my house. Frankly, I was quite astonished that Philip could tolerate being with him. Yet here they were going about together like a couple of lifelong pals. Even their coats were identical.

The reason the drumming sound had seemed familiar, of course, was because I'd previously heard it at Steve's house. He found it almost impossible to sit still, so he would pass the minutes by drumming with his fingers on the table, or whatever other surface happened to be nearby. The last time I'd been to see him was to collect some sugar he'd borrowed some months earlier and hadn't returned. He insisted that I stayed for a while, then subsequently drove me half-mad with this incessant drumming.

When he wasn't doing that he was rushing round making so-called improvements to his house. It was similar to mine in many respects, built entirely from tin, yet for some reason he was never quite satisfied with it. As a consequence, there was always some half-finished job under way: shutters on and off their hinges; the chimney lengthened or shortened; the stairs rebuilt. On the occasion of that last visit he'd been engaged in fixing a weathercock on the roof, a task with which I somehow became involved. I lost count of how many times I had to hold his ladder while he went up to make adjustments, but at the end of the day he still wasn't happy with the result.

Another thing I remembered about Steve was that he

tended to leave his door open for long periods, which allowed masses of sand to be blown inside his house. He didn't seem the slightest bit bothered by this and traipsed it all around the place. I knew very well that Mary Petrie would frown on such carelessness, so as soon as he arrived I made a mental note to keep an eye on him.

Philip, on the other hand, was much more of a stalwart figure who could be trusted to leave doors firmly closed. On the few occasions I'd been to his house, everything had been battened down securely against inclement weather. He had never struck me as the type who would be easily given to running round on half-baked schemes of the sort favoured by Steve. Nonetheless, the two of them seemed to get on very well together, so I didn't question their friendship.

As they sat there at the table, with Steve already beginning to drum his fingers, I wondered what they'd come over for. Neither of them owed me anything, nor I them, and as far as I knew they weren't in the habit of making calls just for the sake of saying hello. That was much more in Simon Painter's line than theirs. The only other motive I could think of for the visit was that they wanted some sort of favour. I decided, therefore, that the best course of action was to make breakfast, and let them choose their moment.

'House is looking good,' remarked Philip, as he peered around the interior.

'Yes,' I replied. 'I try to keep it ship-shape.'

'Hmm hmm,' he murmured.

'Probably be giving it a good spring-clean once this wind's dropped.'

'Hmm.'

He wasn't the most talkative of people.

'How's your place these days?' I asked.

'Same as ever,' he answered.

'Tell him about your new weathercock,' suggested Steve.

'Oh, yes,' said Philip. 'I've got a new weathercock.'

For a second I thought he might expand on the subject, but instead he merely fell silent. Meanwhile his companion continued drumming on the table top. A violent gust of wind made the whole house creak, which in turn caused both of them instantly to glance towards the stairway. Then they looked expectantly in my direction, and I realized all at once why they'd come.

'Everything alright?' I asked, smiling.

'Yes, yes,' replied Steve. 'Fine.'

'OK then,' I said. 'I'll start breakfast. Make yourselves at home.'

'Thanks.'

The preparations took about twenty minutes, during which time soft footsteps could be heard moving around on the upper floor. However, I gave no sign of having noticed them.

When breakfast was almost ready I said, quite casually, 'Would one of you mind laying the table?'

'I'll do it,' said Steve, practically leaping to his feet.

He went and got some cutlery out of the drawer, and there then followed a long pause.

'How many places shall I set?' he asked at length.

'Three of course,' I replied. 'Why?'

'Is there no one else joining us then?'

'Don't know,' I said.

'Oh . . . er, right.'

'I suppose you could lay an extra one if you want to, though, just in case.'

'OK then.'

He busied himself around the table and finished laying it in seconds. Then I served up breakfast and the three of us began to eat.

'You never can tell,' I remarked, nodding towards the empty place. 'Sometimes she does, sometimes she doesn't.'

As I finished the sentence I noticed that my two guests' eyes had suddenly swivelled towards the stairs, and next thing Mary Petrie had come down.

'Aha,' I said. 'Here's a nice surprise.'

Without saying a word she passed behind my seat and slapped me hard on the back of the head. Then, in the stunned silence that followed, she poured herself a coffee and went back upstairs.

'Friend of yours?' asked Steve, keeping his voice low.

'Yes,' I replied, equally quietly. 'She's been here a few months now.'

'That's what we heard.'

'From Simon Painter?'

'Yes,' he said. 'Does she do that often?'

'No,' I said. 'First time.'

'Well, I wouldn't stand for it.'

'Wouldn't you?'

'No, I certainly would not.'

'Nor me,' said Philip.

I looked at these two men sitting at my table: these two men who'd each spent the last few years living alone in a house of tin, and I realized that they knew even less about women than I did.

'Tell you what,' I said. 'Help yourselves to more coffee, and I'll go up and sort this out.'

'Alright,' answered Steve. 'But take care.'

When I got upstairs Mary Petrie was sitting on the bed leafing through one of her books. She kept these in her trunk because I hadn't got round to putting up a shelf yet.

'It's Steve Treacle and Philip Sibling,' I said.

'So I gather,' she replied, without looking up.

'Don't you want to meet them?'

'Why should I?'

'Cos they've come especially to see you.'

'I don't care!' she snapped. 'I'm not here for display purposes you know!'

'Shush!' I whispered. 'They'll hear you.'

'Don't shush me! They shouldn't have banged on the wall with that hammer.'

'No, that wasn't them.'

'What!?'

Just then the door was heard to open, and two pairs of feet trooped outside before it closed again.

'It was me who banged on the wall,' I explained. 'I was teaching Steve a lesson for waking us up.'

'Well, you're as stupid as he is then.'

Her tone had softened slightly.

'Are you going to come down and see them?' I tried.

'No,' she said. 'I'm not in the mood.'

'They'll be ever so disappointed.'

'Tell them to come back another time, and knock on the door properly.'

'OK.'

I dashed downstairs to intercept them, thinking they might have taken offence and left. When I got outside, however, Steve was busy shovelling sand while Philip stood watching.

'Sorry about that,' I said. 'It's sorted out now.'

'Hmm hmm,' murmured Philip.

'She says you're welcome to come and see us, but it's a bit inconvenient today, if you don't mind.'

'No, no,' said Steve. 'That's fine. I'll just finish clearing this sand, then we'll be getting off.'

'Well, I can do the sand myself,' I said. 'Don't worry about it.'

'It's no problem,' he replied. 'Just you relax, and I'll have it done in no time.'

*   *   *

The pair of them returned a week later, and this time they came bearing gifts. Arriving at a civilized hour in the middle of the morning, they knocked gently on the door and waited to be invited in.

The gifts, they seemed to think, were the reason Mary Petrie gave them a friendly welcome, enquired about their health, and asked them to take a seat at the table. Little did they know that I'd spent the intervening days convincing her that they were two of the finest fellows I had ever known, and that therefore she shouldn't treat them too harshly. They had no idea of the continual praise I'd heaped upon them, and the way I'd kept her entertained with hilarious stories of their various exploits. Gradually she had warmed to them, by proxy, and when I'd reminded her that they both wore identical coats she'd said she thought they sounded 'quite sweet'. As a matter of fact, she finally conceded, she was rather looking forward to seeing them again. The gifts, if they'd known the truth, were merely icing on a cake I'd already made.

To my dismay we received a clock from Philip, while Steve presented us with a weathercock. This was similar to the one on top of his own house, and a little later he went outside to see if he could recommend a good place to fix it. Philip accompanied him.

'I don't want a weathercock,' I said, once they were out of earshot. 'I've lived here long enough to know which way the wind's blowing without having to look. It's west-south-west most of the time and hardly ever varies. What do I need with a weathercock when there's a prevailing wind?'

'Well, I think it's very kind of him,' replied Mary Petrie. 'And a clock from Philip!'

'That's even worse.'

'Why?'

'You know I don't like clocks.'

'Oh don't start that again,' she said. 'Look, you asked me to be nice to them, and I'm trying to be, but now you're being rude about their presents. Snap out of it, why don't you?'

'Well, why do people always bring these things that are supposed to be useful but in fact aren't?'

'I don't know,' she answered. 'They're your friends.'

Just then we heard the sound of feet tramping about overhead.

'Great,' I said. 'They're on the roof now.'

This was just the sort of behaviour I'd been hoping they would avoid, at least on their first official visit. I'd have thought it was obvious from the previous week that they had to be careful what they did, yet here they were clambering around above us within half an hour of arriving! I suppose it was the consequence of living alone for so many years. Steve and Philip were both free to do more or less what they wanted in their own homes, and had no concept of the sort of domestic life that I was slowly getting used to. If they carried on like this much longer they were likely to make themselves less than welcome.

'That's what I've noticed about your friends,' said Mary Petrie. 'For some reason they all like going up on our roof.'

This was the first time I'd heard her refer to the roof as 'ours'.

'Well, I hope they don't leave any dents up there,' I remarked. 'It's not for walking about on.'

We went outside and saw our two guests perched high up and not looking particularly safe.

'What are you doing up there?' I asked, in the friendliest tone I could muster.

'Just reconnoitring really,' replied Steve. 'There's a good few fixing places: we're trying to find the best one.'

'Be careful, won't you!' called Mary Petrie.

I had to admit she was going out of her way to be agreeable towards them. She appeared genuinely concerned as the two intrepids helped each other down over the eaves, found footholds on the shutters, then finally dropped to the ground.

'We'll need a ladder to do the job properly,' said Philip. 'Have you got one?'

'No,' I replied. ''Fraid not.'

'You'll have been up on the roof before though, surely?'

'Actually, no I haven't.'

'Never been on the roof?' He looked quite surprised.

'No.'

'So you didn't know you could see Simon Painter's house from up there?'

'Oh, yes,' I said. 'I knew that: he told me.'

'You can hear his bell jangling sometimes too,' added Mary Petrie.

'Pity no one heard his cries for help,' said Steve. 'You know he was blocked in by the sand for five days?'

'Was he?'

'Yes, if we hadn't rescued him he'd still be there now.'

'Blimey, I didn't know that.'

'Poor Simon!' said Mary Petrie. 'As if he hasn't got enough worries.'

I looked at her and wondered what these other worries were supposed to be. As far as I was concerned it wasn't 'Poor Simon!' but 'I told you so!'

I'd said all along that his door opened the wrong way and he was going to get blocked in if he wasn't careful, but no one would listen. I was even barred from discussing the subject in my own house! Now, however, everyone was standing round sympathizing with Simon as though his fate was completely out of his hands.

7

We were still talking about Simon Painter that afternoon when we sat down at the table for tea. It transpired in the conversation that he'd decided to call his house 'Sandfire', and now had a nameplate fixed to the outer wall.

'What does he want to name his house for?' I asked.

'No particular reason as far as I know,' replied Steve. 'I think he just likes the sound of it.'

'You've got to admit it's a nice name,' said Mary Petrie.

'Yes, it is,' I agreed. 'But I still can't see the point of giving a house a name.'

'I think it's all due to Michael Hawkins,' remarked Philip.

'What's he got to do with it?'

'Well, apparently Simon's been out there several times now, and feels very strongly influenced by Michael.'

Straightaway I felt my hackles rising.

'What do you mean *out there*?' I demanded.

'Well,' said Philip with a shrug. 'Michael lives further out than the rest of us, doesn't he?'

'No, he doesn't!' I said. 'We all live a long way out, compared with most people!'

I was aware that my voice had suddenly become louder, and that all three of them were looking at me with startled expressions on their faces. With some effort I spoke more quietly. 'Anyway, what's all this about him influencing Simon?'

'It's the way Michael lives,' said Steve. 'He has this sort of perfect existence, very simple, in a house built entirely from tin, and he passes his time doing many interesting things.'

'Such as?'

'For example, he gets up early to watch the sunrise.'

'You can do that here,' I said.

'I know,' replied Steve. 'But according to Simon it's *different* out there.'

'He's thinking of moving house,' added Philip.

'What, so he can be nearer to this Michael Hawkins person?'

'Apparently, yes.'

I sighed and shook my head incredulously.

'Well, I think it's good that Simon's found some sense of purpose at last,' said Mary Petrie. 'There's nothing for him round here.'

'And what's wrong with *round here* exactly?' I asked.

'There's no use telling you,' she answered. 'You'd never listen.'

'I agree with Mary,' said Steve. 'Simon would be much happier if he made a new start. He just needs a bit of a push, that's all.'

'What sort of push?'

'You know,' he said. 'Encouragement. A step in the right direction.'

I could hardly believe what I was hearing. To my ears, all this talk about 'influence' and 'encouragement' sounded like nothing short of treason. What had happened, I wondered, to the independent lives we'd all enjoyed until so recently? Hadn't we been content, living the way we chose here on this bleak and deserted plain? I'd always presumed the answer was yes, but now I wasn't so certain. Just of late, it seemed, disaffection had arisen amongst us.

I was also bothered by a fact that I'd only vaguely recognized before today, namely, that each of us was beginning to get closely involved with someone else. Rather too closely for my liking. As the four of us sat around the table I suddenly realized that we were no longer three men and a woman discussing the exploits of a mutual friend. Instead, we were two couples analysing his problems. I looked at the clock, newly secured to the wall above our heads, and saw that our future as individuals was ticking irredeemably away.

Meanwhile, there were more mundane matters at hand: the weathercock had to be fixed on the roof. A ladder was clearly required to do the job properly, and so Steve offered to go home and collect his. It was arranged that he and Philip would stay overnight with us, then he'd set off alone early in the morning.

'You'll have to sleep downstairs tonight,' Mary Petrie told me while we were sorting out the spare sheets and blankets.

'Why's that?' I asked.

'Well,' she replied. 'What will those two think of me if I just let you jump into my bed?'

'What will they think of *me* if you don't?' I protested, but I knew there was no point in arguing. Her mind was made up, and that was that. I had to spend the night sleeping alongside Steve and Philip. True, we were all in separate beds, but nevertheless we were close enough together to be easily mistaken for three sardines in a tin can.

Next morning, very early, I rose and made some coffee while Steve got dressed. Then the two of us sat by the stove, listening to the wind howling outside.

'Doesn't sound as if it's dying off yet,' he said, in a quiet voice.

'Well, it never dies altogether,' I reminded him. 'It could blow all spring and summer for all we know.'

'Hope not,' he replied. 'Philip and I want to get out and about a bit more this year.'

'Out and about where?'

'Well, we thought we might mosey over and see Michael Hawkins for a start.'

'You as well?'

'Yes, why not?'

'No, it's alright,' I said. 'Do as you please.'

'Have you got something against Michael?'

'Of course not.'

'I mean, you ought to give him a chance before you judge him.'

'Yes, OK,' I said. 'You're probably right.'

Shortly afterwards Steve finished his coffee, put on his coat and left. I went back to bed but for some reason I couldn't fall asleep again. As the sand scuffed against the outside wall I lay thinking about what he'd said. Maybe I was being a bit unfair on this Michael Hawkins. After all, I'd never even met the man. As daylight came I resolved to try to forget about him and carry on with my own life. Therefore I got dressed, took the shovel and spent an enjoyable couple of hours clearing away the sand. Then I went inside, had breakfast, and waited for Steve's return.

This must have been round about noon. It was a bit too early for lunch, but as he'd been on the move since before dawn Mary Petrie offered to rustle him up something to eat while Philip and I did the weathercock. This arrangement was all good and well, and should have worked to everyone's satisfaction had Steve not been such an impetuous person. The trouble was, he considered himself to be something of an expert at erecting weathercocks, having already put up his own and Philip's. As a result, halfway through his meal he suddenly rushed out of the house to give us some advice. I knew that Mary Petrie wouldn't have been best pleased about this, but I was hardly entitled to order him back in. Besides, I was fully occupied holding the ladder steady for Philip.

'It's got to be dead vertical on its axis!' Steve shouted. 'Otherwise it won't work!'

'Alright!' came the reply from the roof. 'Why don't you go back in and finish your lunch?'

'And make sure it can spin freely!'

'Alright!'

At that moment I noticed Mary Petrie appear in the doorway with an indignant look on her face. I also realized that Steve had left the door wide open. Some sand was already starting to blow into the house, so Mary Petrie took the broom and began tentatively to sweep it away. From my place at the foot of the ladder it still looked as though the day could be saved if Steve would only go back inside and apologize for his absence. Instead, he decided to take command of events, seizing the broom from Mary Petrie and thrusting at the small pile of sand.

'You've obviously never swept up before,' he said, and instantly her eyes were ablaze.

'Don't "obviously" me!' she cried. 'I don't want sand flying about!'

'It won't matter when I've got it outside!' Steve answered, brushing even harder, so that the sand flew upwards.

'Stop it!'

'Hold tight, Philip!' I called, abandoning the ladder and rushing over to the door. I grabbed the broom from Steve just as Mary Petrie went inside and ran upstairs, her face dark with anger. 'You've done it now,' I murmured. 'Why didn't you just eat your lunch?'

'Bit hysterical isn't she?' replied Steve.

'Keep your voice down!'

'Well, I was only showing her how to sweep.'

'Look!' I snapped. 'Leave it!'

I led Steve by the arm and sat him down at the table to finish eating. Then I went back out and steadied the ladder for Philip, who was complaining loudly from the rooftop. We spent another half-hour getting the weathercock properly positioned, during which time Steve emerged from the house and gave his solemn approval. Philip then came down the ladder and we all went inside to warm up a bit. Meanwhile, Mary Petrie remained silent and brooding upstairs.

The three of us sat round the table, drinking coffee, speaking in quiet tones and generally keeping our voices down. Steve and Philip seemed to understand that they would have to leave fairly soon, to give me the opportunity to sort things out. Occasionally one of them would glance at the ceiling, raise his eyebrows and wince as if expecting a mighty blow to fall. In truth, though, they had no idea of the gravity of the situation. Eventually, late in the afternoon, they took their ladder and departed. I accompanied them for half a mile or so. Little was said on that short journey, but I noticed their steps lightened the further they got away from the house.

'Well, I'll say goodbye now,' I said at last. 'I'll be seeing you sometime.'

'OK then,' replied Philip. 'Look after yourself.'

As we parted I shook both their hands, giving Steve an extra crush for good measure. Then I headed home to face the music. It would all be my fault, of course, I knew that.

Pushing open the door I saw Mary Petrie standing at the top of the stairs.

'Right,' she said. 'From now on all your friends are banned.'

'All of them?'

'Yes.'

'How long for?'

'Always.'

By this time, of course, I'd resigned myself to sanctions of some kind or other. I accepted the severity of the verdict without argument, knowing it would all blow over in a week or two. It was impossible for Mary Petrie to enforce a lifetime ban on my friends and acquaintances, that was obvious, so I only had to ride out the storm until the day's events were forgotten. Besides, I thought, it would do no harm to cut down on all the friendly coming and going that had lately been endemic at my house, and which was starting to get out of hand.

Indeed, here was an opportunity to return to how things were before. With a great show of contrition I carefully cleared all the sand out of the house, closed the door, and settled down for a period of relative quiet. I didn't venture upstairs that night, but by the following day the two of us were again talking freely. Late in the afternoon Mary Petrie came outside with me to admire the new weathercock, which, she agreed, looked quite nice. I made no remarks about how unnecessary it was, nor did I point out that the wind showed no sign of abating. Instead I played the part to which I had become accustomed, in which a man remains master of his own home, so long as he observes all the rules.

An uneventful week passed by. Then another. Finally, one morning there was a knock on the door. It was Simon Painter, and he was almost in tears.

'Can you come and help?' he said. 'Someone's taken my house to pieces.'

8

He was a forlorn sight, standing there in the doorway holding his overnight bag. He looked tired, as if he'd been travelling for several hours, and there were traces of red sand on his clothing.

'What do you mean, taken to pieces?' I asked.

'It's been dismantled bit by bit,' he replied. 'And now it's just a pile of tin. What am I going to do?'

He was clearly very desperate.

'Sorry, Simon,' I said. 'I'd like to help but I'm barred from seeing my friends.'

'Don't talk nonsense,' said Mary Petrie, moving me aside. 'Come in out of the cold, Simon, and we'll make you some breakfast.'

'Oh, thank you,' he said. 'You're so kind.'

'How would you like it if it happened to you?' she hissed after he'd gone in.

'Just obeying orders,' I shrugged.

She soon had him sitting down at the table with a hot cup of coffee, and once he'd recovered a little he told us what had happened.

'I don't know if you've heard,' he began, 'but I've been out to stay at Michael Hawkins's place quite a few times lately.'

'Yes,' replied Mary Petrie. 'We'd heard that.' (I understood from the look she gave me that I wasn't allowed to pass comment on the subject.)

'Well, I was there until quite late last night,' he continued. 'Couldn't drag myself away until the small hours, but the moon was out – did you see the moon?'

'No, we didn't.'

'Marvellous, it was, very shiny, so I decided to travel home by moonlight. We do things like that at Michael's: getting up early, staying up late, it's all part of daily life out there.' He paused and took a deep breath. This was followed by a sigh. 'Anyway, as I drew nearer I expected to see the outline of my house appear ahead of me, but instead there was nothing. It was dawn when I got to where it should have been, and all that remained was this big pile of tin, with the flagpole lying nearby.'

'What about your captive balloon?' I asked.

'They've let it down.'

He was beginning to look tearful once more, so Mary Petrie put her arm round his shoulder and said, 'There, there, you'll soon put it together again.'

'I don't know how,' he moaned.

'Well, we'll help, won't we?'

She eyed me firmly, and I realized I was going to have a busy few days ahead.

'Yes, of course,' I said. 'We'll have a nice breakfast, and then we'll go and see what can be done.'

To tell the truth, by the time we were ready to leave I was quite looking forward to the project. It would be a fruitful pastime, I thought, reassembling someone's house, and thereby earning their eternal gratitude. Of course, when Mary Petrie had said we'd help she actually meant me. For her part, she knew nothing about building from tin, and would have been no use at all. Actually, I knew nothing either, but I assumed it would be fairly straightforward.

Mary Petrie saw us off after breakfast, and said she might have a walk across later to see how we were getting on. Meanwhile, she'd have some space to herself, which would be an agreeable change for her. By now I was pleased to see that Simon was getting some of his bounce back, and as we approached his place we shared a general feeling of optimism.

This disappeared the moment we saw the enormity of the job. I had expected it to be quite obvious which piece went where, but when we were confronted by that huge pile of tin I was frankly dumbfounded. How were we supposed to tell the roof from the walls, the back from the front, and so on? The only readily identifiable parts were the door, the shutters and the chimney, which had been carefully set to one side.

'Considerate of someone,' I remarked, as we stood surveying the ruins. 'They've even folded up your balloon.'

There didn't seem to be any malice attached to the dismantling of Simon Painter's house. I mean to say, anybody who wished to destroy it would have been better off using dynamite. Instead they'd simply taken it to pieces and left it in a heap. There was a separate stack which turned out to be all his worldly goods, neatly bundled together so as not to come to any harm.

'You didn't leave the door locked then?' I asked in passing.

'Of course not,' replied Simon. 'There was no need . . . normally.'

I could see he was quite upset, so I decided the best thing would be to get started immediately, in order to keep his mind occupied.

Where to begin, though? It was like attempting to solve a jigsaw puzzle that had come in a box without an illustration on the lid.

'We should have brought that picture you gave me,' I said. 'You haven't got another one anywhere have you?'

'There's one on the bedroom wall.'

'Well,' I said. 'At least that's a clue: we'll start there.'

I approached the pile of tin and began going through it in search of the piece with the picture attached. Deep inside, though, it felt like a hopeless task. Even if we did find part of his bedroom wall, how on earth were we going to build the rest of the house around it?

'I'm sorry I can't offer you a coffee,' said Simon. 'The stove won't work without the chimney.'

'Not to worry,' I replied. 'What about lighting a fire out in the open? That'll cheer us up a bit.'

'No fuel,' he said. 'I've spent so much time at Michael's lately that it's completely run down.'

'Blimey, you have got it bad haven't you?'

'Suppose so.'

'Hello,' I said. 'Here comes the cavalry.'

There were two figures moving towards us in the distance, and as they drew nearer I recognized Steve and Philip. Then all at once they started running.

'Don't touch the tin!' shouted Steve, as soon as he was close enough. 'Each piece is specially marked!'

'Alright!' I called back. 'We've only moved a few!'

They dashed up and began manhandling the pile until it was more or less back to how it had been before. Meanwhile, Simon stood and watched them in stunned silence.

'This and this are right,' said Steve as he attended to the last pieces. 'But that has to be put on top of there.' He and Philip heaved a long section of tin onto the pile, then turned and looked at Simon with an air of satisfaction.

'Righto,' announced Steve. 'You're all ready to get moving.'

'Moving where?' Simon asked.

'Towards Michael Hawkins's, of course.'

'You mean move my house there?'

'Yes.'

'Oh . . . I see.'

Simon's reaction was interesting, because instead of exploding with rage at Steve and Philip's audacity, he just stood there blinking as the idea sunk in.

'Is this the "encouragement" you were talking about the other day?' I asked. 'A "bit of a push"?'

'Yep,' said Steve.

'And you never thought to consult Simon first?'

'Nope.'

'I suppose we should have really,' remarked Philip. 'When you come to think about it.'

'No, it's alright,' said Simon, suddenly breaking his silence. 'It's a marvellous thing you've done, setting me on a path I should have taken a long while ago. Thank you both! Yes, I will move. I'll build my house within a mile of Michael.'

At this moment I thought it wise not to set forth my own opinion on the matter. Nonetheless, I was surprised at the ease with which Simon accepted his new circumstances. Here he was being practically evicted by a pair of well-meaning neighbours, yet he talked as if it was part of his destiny. I'd already noticed how he adopted a very solemn tone of voice whenever he spoke of Michael Hawkins. Now, it seemed, he was prepared to stake everything on their friendship.

'How are you going to get it all budged?' I asked.

'Simple,' replied Steve. 'We'll take it one piece at a time.'

Apparently he and Philip had been planning all this for a good while. They'd known in advance that Simon would be away for a couple of days, and as soon as he'd departed they'd come over. Then the pair of them had gone all round the house, marking each section with chalk before dismantling it, so it would be easy to assemble again. This had been a two-day job. Having finished the work late on the previous evening, they'd popped over to Philip's for supper and bed, planning to return in the morning and surprise Simon. As it was, he'd decided to travel overnight and had got back sooner than expected, which is why he'd wound up in a distraught state at my place.

'All the chalk marks correspond,' explained Steve. 'So as long as we keep the pieces in order, we'll have the whole outfit back together in no time.'

'When shall we start?' asked an eager Simon.

'Soon as you like.'

While the three of them stood planning the expedition, I went and had a quiet look at the chalk markings. Sure enough, each part of the house bore an inscription, such as TRH, LHT or FRS. I couldn't make head or tail of any of it, but I guessed that Steve had the method of assembly all worked out, and therefore I enquired no further.

By this time they'd agreed to set off immediately with the first few pieces. Simon had now thought of a possible site to establish his new home, and he estimated that it would take about five hours to get there.

'We can stay at Michael's tonight,' he said. 'Then come back for some more bits tomorrow.'

'If we go via my place we can stop for a meal on the way,' suggested Steve. Then he looked at me. 'Unless, of course, you'd prefer your own cuisine?'

'How do you mean?' I asked.

'Well, if you want to nip home first we'll wait for you.'

I gathered from this remark that they assumed I was going with them, which, of course, I wasn't. In my view it was one thing to turn out and help someone get over a little local difficulty, but quite another to spend several days moving a tin house overland.

'Actually, I won't be coming,' I said. 'I'll stay here and be quartermaster instead.'

'Quartermaster?' asked Steve.

'Yes, you know, I'll look after the pieces while you're away. Stop them being stolen, that kind of thing.'

'There's no one here except us,' he replied. 'Who's going to steal them?'

'Well, they might get blown around.'

'Alright,' he said. 'If you're not interested it doesn't matter.'

Without further word he walked away to join the others, leaving me feeling a little awkward. Subsequent conversation was held only between the three of them as they prepared for their forthcoming journey. A little later they set off, each bearing part of a house of tin.

No one said goodbye. Not even Simon.

9

I stayed there for a long time after they'd gone, reluctant to leave the remaining pile unguarded. I knew as well as they did that this was quite unnecessary, for as Steve had pointed out, there was no one around except us. Even so, I felt obliged to make certain everything was secure. A length of rope lay coiled amongst Simon's possessions, and I used it to tie down all the various pieces. This, I assured myself, would protect them from the wind. Then, when I was satisfied there was no more I could do, I headed for home. Halfway back I met Mary Petrie. She was carrying a basket in her hand.

'That was quick work,' she said. 'Have you put Simon together already?'

'Not quite,' I replied. 'He's decided to move.'

The basket contained a flask of coffee, along with some cakes which she'd brought to keep us going. I told her what had happened, and how the others had left without saying goodbye.

'Well,' she remarked. 'At least you've still got me, haven't you?'

This was one way of looking at it, of course, but as we returned home I couldn't help thinking that I might never see my friends again. After all, they had little cause to come calling any more. These thoughts played on my mind quite a lot that night. By the following morning I'd resolved to go over to Simon Painter's place every day with a basket of provisions for the three of them. Then they'd know that although they were gone, they were by no means forgotten. For some reason, however, I couldn't face seeing them in person. This wasn't because I felt ashamed for not helping with the move. It was just that I didn't think I'd know what to say to any of them. Accordingly, I decided not to pay my visit until the late afternoon, by which time I reckoned they should have arrived and departed again.

Sure enough, when I got to Simon's about an hour before dusk the first thing I noticed was that three more pieces of tin had been taken away. I was pleased to see they'd used the rope to tie down the rest of the pile, just as I had, but apart from that there was no sign of anyone having been there. I checked everything was secure, then left the basket of victuals in a prominent position.

When I went back the next day the pile had again been reduced by three items. It was disappointing to discover, though, that the flask of coffee had not been touched. Only the cakes were gone.

'Perhaps the coffee went cold overnight,' suggested Mary Petrie when she heard about it.

Of course, I thought, how stupid of me! After that I switched to making my delivery early in the morning, then returning again in the afternoon to retrieve the basket. This system was quite time-consuming, involving two journeys there and back, but I felt somehow rewarded the first time I found the coffee had been drunk and all the cakes eaten.

As the days went by I found that these trips became increasingly important to me. I would study closely the diminishing stack of tin to see which pieces had been removed, and always I looked to see if anything new had been left behind. There was nothing I was expecting in particular, I should add, but I thought I might find an occasional message saying how they were getting on, or maybe a 'thank you' note. Instead, there was only the empty basket. It soon became clear that my daily offerings were of little importance compared with the task of moving an entire house bit by bit. This did little, however, to reduce my interest, which was now starting to become obsessive. I began to recognize the ways in which the pieces of tin had been marked for reassembly, and I kept a note of them for my own reference. I'd soon worked out, for example, that FRS was an abbreviation of *front right side*, while LHT meant *left hand top*. The more I became acquainted with this special code Steve Treacle had devised, the more I suspected that it was doomed to failure. My doubts were confirmed when I came across a part marked TLH. What was the difference, I wondered, between *top left hand* and *left hand top*?

After two weeks the pile had decreased considerably in size. Still the coffee and cakes were consumed daily, and still I received no acknowledgement. Undeterred, I maintained my regular visits. This soon caused trouble at home. Mary Petrie mentioned frequently that I seemed to be spending a lot of time away, so one afternoon I invited her to come with me on my journey. Then she could find out for herself what was so fascinating about a heap of tin, as she put it. We arrived quite late because of the speed she walked, then all she did was stand gazing in silence at the deserted site. This was actually her first visit to Simon

Painter's house, and I could see that its reduced condition meant nothing to her. Therefore, I thought I'd better explain the layout.

'Simon used to live right on this very spot,' I said. 'The door was here and the kitchen was there, and the stove was in that corner. Don't you find that interesting?'

'Not if he's left the place, no,' she replied. 'Where's his bell?'

A short search revealed it hidden amongst his other possessions, along with the Sandfire nameplate, the wind chimes and the rolled-up flag. I gave the bell a ring, and when she heard its familiar tone her eyes welled up with tears.

'How come you're so engrossed with Simon all of a sudden?' she demanded. 'When he was living here all you did was criticize him!'

'Yes, but only as a friend,' I replied.

'You were never friendly to him!'

'I was.'

'No you weren't!' she cried. 'And now he's gone and you deserve it!'

Next moment she had turned away and was stalking homeward. I wanted to go after her and find out what fault I was supposed to be guilty of now, but there were one or two things I needed to do first. Quickly I counted the pieces of tin to see what still remained, then I checked the rope was secure, grabbed the basket and set off in pursuit.

It was remarkable how far she'd got in that short time. I judged she'd covered a couple of hundred yards already, which was some distance considering her earlier complaint that she couldn't walk any faster! She marched along with such a determined stride that anyone would have thought she was trying to put as much space between us as possible.

For my part I had no intention of exerting myself just to catch up, so I strolled along at a normal pace, knowing that I was bound to overhaul her eventually. This actually took longer than I'd estimated, and it wasn't until we were nearly home that I got close enough to speak.

'I deserve what, exactly?' I asked.

'You deserve to be left on your own!' replied Mary Petrie.

'What, just because I criticized Simon Painter once or twice?'

'Don't drag Simon into it!' she snapped. 'At least he cares about other people! All you care about is yourself and your silly little house of tin!'

She was still making no effort to slow down, but pressed on with her eyes looking straight ahead. The house in question was now in full view.

'What's silly about it?' I enquired.

'It's all silly! Look at it! Sticking up in the middle of nowhere, miles from anyone else!'

'But that's why it's so perfect!'

'You really believe that, don't you?' she said. 'You really think you're living some sort of enviable existence. That's the reason you keep going over to Simon's all the time: you just can't accept that he could ever dream of moving away. Oh no, there can't be anywhere better than here because this is the centre of the world! Everyone else must be wrong! How can they not want to live on a cold, windy and desolate plain, in a silly little house of tin where you have to shovel sand every morning and bolt the door to stop it flying open?'

Suddenly Mary Petrie stopped in her tracks and faced me.

'I'll tell you why you're here,' she said. 'You're here because you think it makes you different. You think this silly little tinpot life of yours, this self-imposed isolation, makes you more interesting than other people. Don't you? Eh? You're convinced that if everybody had the chance then they too would live in a house built entirely from tin. You can't see that all you're doing is playing, the same as Simon, Steve and Philip were playing before they grew out of it! You're playing at being a loner who can get by without anyone else. That's why you cut yourself off like some recluse! You couldn't find a cabin in a canyon so you chose this place instead. A gleaming, grey, two-storey edifice with a sloping roof and a tin-plate chimney! You believe it's a fortress, but I'll tell you something: it's tinny and it's temporary and one of these days it's going to fall down about your ears!'

When she'd finished speaking she stood glaring at me with her hands on her hips and her eyes ablaze.

I waited a moment and then said, 'So you don't like my corrugated dwelling?'

Mary Petrie sighed. 'You still don't understand,' she said. 'What I mean is, it's not where you are that counts but who you're with.'

'Does that mean I shouldn't go to Simon Painter's any more?'

'Of course not, but try to pay me some attention too.'

'Alright then.'

Her look softened. She sighed again and turned towards the house. I watched as she walked the remaining distance before disappearing inside, then spent a few minutes pondering what she'd said. The gist of it, as far as I could gather, was that the whole place was on the verge of collapse. Obviously I didn't want her to feel insecure, so I gave it a quick examination for structural weakness. As I expected there was nothing wrong at all, but I thought it better not to go inside straightaway as she obviously needed time to herself. Instead, therefore, I waited around while the pale afternoon light began to fade.

This was a time of day I'd always enjoyed, when I could watch the horizon being gradually encroached by gloom. The air felt slightly warmer than usual, suggesting that the wind had veered a little. A glance at the weathercock told the same story. The vane had been pointing steadfastly west-south-west ever since we'd fixed it to the roof. Now, however, it had swung towards Simon Painter's house. In former times this would have allowed the futile clanging of a bell to drift into our hearing. Lately, of course, there was nothing but the moan of the wind, which at last appeared to be losing some of its harshness. There was less sand being borne along with it than usual, and I glanced idly towards the house to see if any needed clearing away. As I did so a distant movement caught my eye. It was far away to the north, where a dense bank of clouds was settling down for the night. I peered into the dimness, trying to work out what I'd seen. Then, after a few more moments had passed, I spied a remote and solitary figure wandering slowly from east to west.

10

Eventually the morning came for my final trip to Simon Painter's. Several more days had gone by, and the pile of tin had continued steadily to diminish. In the end there were just three items left.

Before I set off with the provisions, Mary Petrie said, 'Are you going to try to see them today?'

'I don't think so,' I replied. 'What would we talk about?'

'Well, they're your friends,' she said. 'Surely you can think of something.'

'Not at the moment, I can't, no.'

'So you're going to leave it, are you?'

'Probably.'

'Suit yourself then, but I tell you, you'll regret it.'

Several times recently she'd urged me to time my visits so that I'd be there when they arrived, but unfortunately I still remained unable to face them. In fact, the longer I left it the more difficult it seemed to become. Today, as Mary Petrie was trying to point out, was my last chance to confirm our friendship. After that we were likely to drift even further apart.

Arriving at Simon's, I looked at what was left of his house. Besides the three pieces of tin, the only reminder that it had ever existed was a faint rectangle marked in the sand. His flagpole, the bell and the rest of his personal possessions had been removed on intervening days, and now there was almost nothing. With some misgivings I placed the basket in a safe position, and went home.

When I got back Mary Petrie was still out on her daily walk, so I poured some coffee and went to wait on the doorstep. The wind had continued to lessen during the past week, and there was now little danger of sand coming into the house. As a matter of fact, the weather had taken a general turn for the better. I was almost prepared to say that spring had come at last!

After a while I saw Mary Petrie in the distance. She'd been following her normal circuit of the house, keeping it only just in sight, and now she was on her way back. As a gesture of goodwill I went inside and put some fresh coffee on the stove. When she arrived a few minutes later, it was almost ready.

'I saw some people earlier,' she said. 'Three women, I think, but they were quite a long way off.'

Quickly I moved to the door and looked out.

'Where are they now?' I asked.

'Oh, they'll have gone,' she replied. 'That was about an hour ago.'

'Which direction were they going?'

'It's hard to say really. They looked as if they were just sort of roaming around.'

'Well, which way roughly?'

'I don't know!' she snapped. 'Over there somewhere!'

She waved her arm towards the doorway, which meant anywhere generally to the west.

'Oh,' I said. 'Right.'

I didn't bother to enquire further, because Mary Petrie quite often lost patience if I asked too many questions. A similar thing had happened some months before when she'd come home and told me about an unusual cloud formation she'd noticed. Apparently it resembled a bird, but when I asked if she meant a bird in flight, or just perching, she'd flared up and announced that it didn't matter what sort of bird it was! Furthermore, she said she wouldn't bother to tell me next time she saw anything of interest.

Today's sighting was the same. As far as she was concerned she'd seen some women, they'd gone, and that was that. The subject was closed.

Nevertheless, I was curious about who they could be. It wasn't unusual for people to turn up on the plain from time to time, even in a location as far out as ours. This was mainly much later in the season, though, when the weather had got warm enough to call summer. Such newcomers often pictured themselves as pioneers, or even explorers, just because they happened to be camping in the wilds for a few weeks. Yet as soon as the cold wind returned they'd disappear and wouldn't be seen again.

The three women spotted by Mary Petrie, on the other hand, had arrived within days of winter coming to an end. The same applied for the wandering individual I'd observed the other evening. It struck me that this part of the world was becoming quite crowded for the time of year, and I pondered what was bringing them all in our direction.

*   *   *

'I think we'll have these shutters open,' said Mary Petrie a little later. 'Let some light in for a change.'

This was intended as an instruction to me, of course, and I had to spend an hour or two going round the outside of the house trying to get them all unfastened. In truth, I'd been hoping to avoid the question of the shutters because I knew some of them to be badly jammed. During previous years I'd found it much more convenient simply to prop the door open in mild conditions, and leave the shutters as they were. Mary Petrie had other ideas. Things had to be done correctly, in her opinion, which meant the shutters should be open and the door closed.

When I'd finally completed the task of unjamming catches and getting hinges oiled, it was quite late in the afternoon. For a while I considered not going to Simon Painter's to collect the basket until next morning, but in the end I decided a stroll would be a good idea. There was a gentle breeze blowing throughout the house, not a speck of sand anywhere, and Mary Petrie was busy arranging her vases of dried grass. With a general feeling of well-being I set off on my short journey.

In former times, when I approached Simon Painter's place the first thing I would see would be his captive balloon, followed soon afterwards by the flagpole, the chimney and then the upper part of his roof. These I would register in a casual way as I drew nearer. More recently I had become accustomed to finding a depleted pile of tin waiting for me. Today I expected to see only a basket containing an empty flask. I was surprised, therefore, when I suddenly noticed that there were three people standing where the house used to be.

For a moment I hesitated in my step, thinking it was Simon, Steve and Philip. They were still a good distance away, but I could tell from their movements that they'd already seen me coming. For this reason I felt I had no choice but to continue towards them. It was only then that I saw it was three women. They were all looking at me as I walked up, so I adopted a proprietorial air and headed directly for the basket, which had been placed on the ground nearby.

'Do you want something?' one of them asked, as I picked it up.

'I've just come to collect this,' I replied. 'I brought it here earlier for some friends of mine.'

'But now you're taking it away.'

'Yes,' I said. 'It's empty. Well, it's not actually empty, but it's got an empty flask inside.'

'Where are these friends then?'

'They were moving the house that used to be here. They've gone now.'

It seemed wrong having to explain myself to these three women. After all, they were the strangers, not me. The one who was asking all the questions seemed especially hostile, so I was relieved when another one spoke in a friendlier tone.

'Oh well,' she said. 'I expect you've got as much right to be here as we have.'

'Thanks,' I heard myself say. The three of them seemed to relax slightly, so I carried on the conversation by pointing to the rectangular mark on the ground. 'The house was right here. It was built entirely from tin.'

'So why has the owner moved?' asked the third woman.

'He fancied a change, that's all.'

They glanced at each other, and the second one even managed a smile.

'Good place to live, is it?' she enquired.

'Yes,' I said. 'Great.'

'Cos we're looking for somewhere.'

'Oh, right. Well, you won't find anywhere better than this.'

I then explained in length about how the house had faced west-south-west, which is where the prevailing wind came from, and how I lived about three miles away in one direction, while there were also a couple of other people living further towards the west. Meanwhile they all stood around, gazing at the rectangle, the sky and the horizon. Occasionally they even gazed at me.

When I'd finished speaking, the first one said, 'Where does that go?'

She was pointing at something that had come into existence over the past few weeks, namely, the beginnings of a trail. It followed the route taken each day by Simon, Steve and Philip, and consisted of no more than a collection of footprints. Even so, it appeared to lead to some far-off destination, and I could understand the interest it must have aroused in the three women.

'It doesn't go anywhere really,' I said. 'It's all just wilderness from here.'

'Wilderness?'

'Yes, you know. More of the same.'

In that instant a look passed between them that I wasn't supposed to recognize. It was one of pity, and I knew that for some reason they all felt sorry for me. Awkwardly, I opened the basket as if to check the contents. Then I closed it again. Meanwhile, the three women seemed to have come to an unspoken agreement. Lying on the ground were several bags, which they now began to gather up.

'We'll probably have a look along there,' said the second one, nodding towards the trail. 'Seems quite promising.'

She started walking and the others closed in behind.

'Bye,' I said.

'Bye,' they all replied.

I watched as they went, and wondered what it was they expected to find. Then I picked up the basket, took a last look at the rectangular mark, and started for home. When I got back Mary Petrie was engaged with closing all the shutters for the night. Some of these had been quite difficult to open, and I was impressed with how she was coping on her own. There was only one left to do, so I reached up and held it while she released the catch. Next thing it was securely fastened down.

'Thanks,' she said. 'It's a big improvement having shutters that work.'

'Good,' I replied. 'By the way, I saw those three women you told me about. They were looking at Simon Painter's old place.'

'Thinking of settling there, are they?'

'No,' I said. 'I think they gave it some serious consideration, but in the end they decided to move on.'

'Seeking they know not what,' she remarked, before going inside.

It was dusk now and the gentle breeze of the day was beginning to freshen slightly. Despite my previous objections to having a weathercock on the roof, I'd begun to find it fairly interesting in a casual sort of way, and I tended to glance at it quite often. This evening I noticed that it was still pointing towards the west, as it had done for several days now. For the time being the prevailing wind had ceased, but I was certain this change was only temporary.

11

The opening of the shutters soon became a daily ritual in my house of tin. It was done each morning before breakfast, at the command of Mary Petrie. There were exceptions, of course, such as when the wind gusted up and blew the sand around as if summer had never come. On those occasions the whole place remained firmly battened down. Most days, however, the weather was good. Therefore, the shutters were opened and the light let in.

I had no objection to this as it gave me plenty to do. More importantly, it kept Mary Petrie happy as she continued her improvements to the interior. There were now vases and pictures everywhere, downstairs and up, as well as the further comforts she had produced from her trunk. We drank our coffee, for example, not from enamelled mugs as had long been my custom, but from china cups and saucers. At night we slept beneath a feather eiderdown.

With the shutters open the house was pleasant, bright and airy, yet after a while there appeared an unforeseen side effect. For some reason the increased ventilation caused the stove to emit more smoke than it had previously. Soon there were deposits of soot appearing on the walls, and Mary Petrie demanded that something should be done about it.

'We can't do anything,' I said. 'It's unavoidable.'

'Don't give me that,' she answered, opening the door and going outside. A moment later she was back. 'The chimney's too short. We'll have to have a longer one.'

'Wouldn't it be easier just to close the shutters again?' I suggested. 'That's obviously what's causing it.'

'I don't want them closed!' she exclaimed. 'They're much better open at this time of year. What it needs is a longer chimney!'

'How do you know?'

'I just do!!'

The look on her face confirmed that she was certain of this, so I immediately gave up arguing.

'That must have been why Steve Treacle lengthened his chimney,' I remarked. 'I wondered what he did that for.'

'So he could show you how to do it, could he?' asked Mary Petrie.

'Oh yes, he's got all the stuff over there.'

'Well, you'll have to go and see him then.'

'I can't really, can I?' I protested. 'Not the way things are at present.'

'I don't care about that!' she said. 'I'm not putting up with all this soot when there's a perfectly simple solution! It's only pride that's keeping you away from Steve, and Philip for that matter, so you can get yourself over there tomorrow!'

*　　*　　*

The following day I set forth in the sunshine bearing gifts. I'd decided overnight that there would have to be one for each of my remaining neighbours, and that the best thing to take would be some cakes.

'Won't they have had their fill of cakes by now?' asked Mary Petrie. 'That's what you took every day when they were moving Simon. Maybe you should give them something else instead.'

'No, no,' I replied. 'Cakes'll be fine.'

'Alright,' she said. 'Well, give them both my regards, won't you?'

'OK then. Bye.'

A good while had passed since I'd last been to Steve's, but I was quite sure of the way and hardly even thought about it as I walked. After a couple of hours, however, I began to wonder if maybe I'd strayed off course a little. There was no other landmark in the vicinity apart from Steve's house, and I'd expected it to appear ahead of me at any minute. Instead I saw nothing, so I decided to stop and have a good look around me. The view, I thought, seemed familiar. In all directions a vast red plain stretched away into the distance, crossed occasionally by eddies of drifting sand. Yes, this was definitely the right place.

Where, then, was the house? As I glanced about me my eyes fell on a large rectangular shape marked on the ground, and suddenly I knew the answer. With ease I traced the perimeter of Steve's former abode, recognizing the places where the door, the stove and the stairway used to be. Now it was all gone, and so was the collection of spare parts he kept stacked round the back. These, I recalled, included some lengths of chimney pipe. The whole lot had disappeared, and I could only assume that he'd decided to move nearer to Philip. I wondered if he'd used the same system to notate the pieces of tin from his own house as he had with Simon Painter's. If so, it would be interesting to see the result, which was why I decided to press on in the direction of Philip's. This was only another hour's journey away, and as long as I got a move on I'd have plenty of time to get home again before dark.

After taking what I assumed was my last ever look at Steve Treacle's old residence, I started off. My inhibitions about seeing the two of them again had now disappeared, and I found myself eagerly anticipating the prospect of a pair of tin houses standing side by side. I could just imagine the carry-on when Steve, impetuous as ever, had rushed about reassembling his components right next door to Philip. Meanwhile, his companion would have lent a hand in a staid sort of way, saying little apart from passing the odd droll remark. I speculated that Steve might well have found a method for coupling the two structures together. What a sight that would be, and maybe they'd even have a chimney to spare! Surely, I told myself, when I arrived and presented them both with cakes, the three of us would be able to forget recent events altogether.

During the past hour I'd become aware that the wind had swung back towards west-south-west and was increasing slightly. I felt quite pleased that I'd detected this change without the aid of a weathercock, but something else gratified me as well. To tell the truth, I found the mild, gentle conditions of summer rather irritating, much as I imagined a sailor might feel when stuck in the doldrums. Warm, hazy days were alright for a short period, but after a while I found them frankly tiresome and longed for a return to 'proper weather'. By this I meant louring grey skies, a cool temperature and a bracing wind. A glance at the horizon told me that my wish was about to be granted, although I knew there would be a price to pay. Some regions are simply not suited to summer, and this plain of ours was a perfect example. I'd learnt from experience that we would have to undergo a violent storm before the climate reverted to normal. With this in mind I put my head down and hurried on towards Philip Sibling's house.

It was even longer since I'd been there than it had been for Steve Treacle's, but if I remembered rightly the last occasion was in the aftermath of just such a storm. The previous evening had seen a gathering of clouds in the distance, and sometime around midnight the rain had come. This was a fairly rare occurrence in these parts and quite welcome as the tank could always do with a top-up. It had been falling heavily for an hour or so when I put on some waterproofs and went outside to check that the downpipe was clear. A minute later the sky was lit by the brightest bolt of lightning I'd ever seen. The fork struck the ground somewhere in the vicinity of Philip's house, so the following morning when things were drying up I went over to make sure he was alright.

I should have known he would be, of course. Philip Sibling wasn't the sort of person to go out in a deluge like that, and I found him sitting in his kitchen staring at the ceiling.

'I'm trying to work out if any rain came in last night,' he explained.

'Have you got a leak then?' I asked.

'Oh no. It's tight as a ship.'

'So how could rain get in?'

'Capillary action,' he said, giving me a significant look. 'You can't trust it.'

That was just about the longest talk I ever had with Philip. He was a man of few words, and didn't like to waste them in conversation. This suited me fine, and for the remainder of my visit we sat quietly at his table, sharing a pot of coffee and not exchanging more than the most necessary remarks. Just before I departed, Steve Treacle had arrived, apparently for the same reason as me. Philip invited him in, then all three of us sat together for a while, saying very little, until I decided it was time to leave. Something like a year must have passed since that visit, and now, as I walked once more towards Philip's, I recalled Steve drumming frantically on the table. I could still hear him after I'd said goodbye and gone outside, but I could also hear the pair of them beginning to chat away quite freely. That must have been the day when their friendship first started to flourish, and I had no doubt that they discussed more interesting things than capillary action.

I was interrupted in my thoughts by a faint cry. It came from somewhere up ahead, and reminded me of the plaintive call of a bird on some remote and forsaken strand. Except I knew it wasn't a bird. Stopping in my tracks I peered into the distance, where a group of six or seven people was slowly moving towards the west. They were about a mile away, but I could see that they too had been halted by the cry. A moment later another tiny figure came in sight, apparently running after them. They waited while this individual caught up, and then the whole group clustered together for several minutes before continuing westward again.

As they gradually disappeared from view I watched with an odd feeling of disquiet. These people had made their appearance more or less in the area where Philip lived, yet there was no sign of his house nor Steve's. Surely, I thought, the pair of them can't have just upped and gone. Of all the men I knew, Philip was the last I would have expected to dismantle his dwelling and move it somewhere else. After another quarter of an hour's walking, however, I discovered the truth. There, marked on the ground in front of me, was a large empty rectangle. Beyond it lay a trail of footprints. Overcome with disappointment I sat down and ate the cakes myself.

*　　*　　*

By the time I got home Mary Petrie had been round and closed all the shutters against the oncoming storm. The weathercock pointed west-south-west. So far the breeze had only risen slightly, but already sand was beginning to accumulate against the windward side of the house. As I approached I saw her at work with the shovel, clearing some of it away.

'Don't worry about that now,' I said.

'Well, someone's got to do it,' she answered. 'And you're never here these days.'

'I had to go and see about the chimney, didn't I?'

'That's no excuse. This storm's been building up for hours. You should have come back.' She ceased shovelling and looked at me. 'So where is it then?'

'Where's what?'

'The new chimney.'

'Ah, well,' I explained. 'Steve's moved house. So's Philip. They've gone.'

'Where else did you try?' she asked.

'Nowhere. There isn't anywhere else.'

'Great!' she said. 'You've been out all day and returned with nothing!'

By this time I'd gently removed the shovel from her grasp and taken over the work. Actually, this was a complete waste of energy because when the storm arrived it was just going to blow sand all over the place. Under the circumstances, however, I thought I'd better make a show of doing something. Mary Petrie took position nearby and stood watching me with her arms folded.

'Anyway, the chimney shouldn't be a problem for the moment,' I pointed out. 'Not now the shutters are closed again.'

'I expect you're quite pleased about that, aren't you?' she replied. 'Nice dark sky, blustery wind, sand flying around everywhere. Suits you perfectly, doesn't it?'

I was always impressed when she made remarks like these as she seemed to know my likes and dislikes inside out. It was almost as if she'd studied me in depth and was keeping notes on the subject.

'Never mind,' I said. 'We'll be nice and snug inside the house.'

'But it's the height of summer!' she declared. 'We shouldn't need to be nice and snug!'

'It's only summer by name,' I replied. 'We're right in the middle of the wilds, don't forget.'

'No,' she said. 'I'm sure I won't forget that.'

Carefully she opened the door, slipped inside, and shut it again. The descending gloom now appeared close enough to touch. With it came sporadic flashes of lightning, and these told me that we could expect sand and dust, rather than rain, which would fall elsewhere.

To tell the truth, I quite liked watching the advance of dry lightning, as I called it, when I was assured that I wouldn't get soaked to the skin at any moment. For some reason it was never accompanied by thunder, and instead the only noise came from the rising wind as the sand scattered before it. There was nothing to be gained from further work with the shovel, so I had a rest and observed the sky for another few minutes. Then I went in and joined Mary Petrie. I told her about the group of people I'd seen near Philip's place, and the trail of footprints heading west.

'Do you think it's got anything to do with Michael Hawkins?' she asked.

'Why should it?' I replied.

'Well,' she said. 'There aren't usually this many people coming past are there? Maybe they're going to see him.'

'I doubt it,' I said. 'They're probably just having a look round, that's all.'

Our discussion was interrupted when a heavy gust of wind battered against the house. It was certainly going to be a rough night. With a feeling almost of glee I listened to the familiar noise of the tin walls creaking and groaning under the assault. Another hour and it would sound as if someone outside was hurling sand against them. This was the sort of weather I wanted, and with a bit of luck it would stay the same for weeks, or at least until Mary Petrie forgot about altering the chimney.

Even so, I was quite disturbed by her suggested cause for the sudden influx of newcomers. During the past few months I'd managed to forget all about Michael Hawkins and his supposedly marvellous existence somewhere beyond the horizon. Now he entered my thoughts again, and this time he wouldn't go away. I pictured those people in the afternoon pressing westward when the weather was deteriorating so obviously. There'd been something dogged and imperturbable about their progress, and it had shown even in the patience with which they'd awaited the straggler. He in turn had sounded desperate to join them.

Then there was the question of Steve Treacle and Philip Sibling. They had both spoken several times of going to see Michael Hawkins, and I began to wonder if that was in fact where they'd gone. On balance I agreed it was a possibility, but all the same it seemed a bit extreme taking their houses along too.

I was given further cause for conjecture the following day when the brunt of the storm had passed. Emerging quite early in the morning, the first thing I saw was yet another bunch of people in the distance, again heading west. I got the strong impression that for some reason they were giving a wide berth to my place. Their circumspection suited me, of course, as I didn't want strangers coming past at all hours.

What I didn't realize was that this was just the beginning. That afternoon I spotted another person, far away to the south, making his way in the same direction as the others. From then on the sightings became increasingly frequent. Almost every day Mary Petrie would return from her walk and report that she'd seen more travellers going by, sometimes in pairs or on their own, but most often in groups. I saw them too, and I found their movements quite interesting to watch. It was the manner in which they just kept on going that fascinated me, always at the same relentless pace, rarely pausing unless someone had fallen behind, and never changing course. Invariably it was towards the west.

There was something else I noticed as well. Often they moved in single file, one after the other, and when they did I could see that many of them were carrying burdens. At such a distance I couldn't tell for sure, but these looked very much like pieces of tin.

12

I didn't really like going on the roof, not if I could help it. It seemed a bit high to me, and I'd actually never been up there before. Nonetheless, one afternoon I found myself clambering round on top of the house as if it was second nature. This was all to do with the chimney, of course, and Mary Petrie's insistence that it still needed lengthening.

'No point in doing it yet,' I said, when she raised the subject. 'It's practically autumn now and we won't be opening the shutters till spring.'

'Oh yes, and then you'll find another excuse to put it off,' she replied. 'I want it done now.'

'We haven't got a ladder.'

'Look!' she snapped. 'Do you want me to go up there and sort it out myself?'

'No, no,' I said. 'I'll take care of it.'

I wasn't sure how I was going to lengthen it exactly, but I decided that if I went on the roof and carried out an examination, then she'd probably be satisfied for the time being. Having seen Simon, Steve and Philip all go up there without a ladder, I knew it must be possible. I waited until

she'd gone for a walk, however, before I tried. To my astonishment I found it quite easy once I'd managed to scramble
over the eaves, and by the time she came back I was an
accomplished climber. I made sure she saw me at work
with a tape measure, checking the length of the chimney
against its diameter, as well as taking a note of the circum-
ference. Then I tried to get down, and found I couldn't.

She'd already gone inside when I made this discovery.
The trouble was, when I dangled my foot over the eaves I
couldn't find anywhere to place it. At the same time I felt
sudden beads of sweat developing all over my body. I sat
there trying to keep calm and puzzling how the others had
found it so easy. When I thought about it I realized they
were simply more used to it than I was, especially Steve,
who'd done countless alterations to his house. It just needed
practice, that was all, so after a while I tried again. It was
no good, though. The moment I began my descent the beads
of sweat returned and I had to go back up. Now I was
certain I was stuck.

Just then my eye was caught by the sight of some travellers in the distance. Such people had become so common-
place over recent weeks that if I'd seen them from the
ground I'd have barely given them a second glance. From
high up here on the roof, however, they appeared in a new
perspective, and therefore held my gaze a little longer. Long
enough, in fact, for me to notice that they weren't heading
west, as I would have expected, but directly towards me.

Peering more intently I saw that there were three of
them, and that they were walking single file in the steadfast
purposeful way I'd come to recognize amongst these
migrants. Why, I wondered, were they coming to my place?
I was about to call Mary Petrie and warn her when something about the first of the three attracted my attention. At

the same instant I knew it was Simon Painter. Behind him strode Steve Treacle and Philip Sibling.

The effect of seeing my former friends was to propel me onto my feet, completely forgetful of my fear of heights, and turn away from them. They were sufficiently far off for me to pretend not to have seen them coming, so I fumbled in my pocket for the tape and then proceeded to take all sorts of measurements around the roof. I recorded, for example, the dimensions along the eaves, the rise of the roof above the gutters, and the distance between the gables. I continued like this for another ten minutes or so, all the time making sure I never glanced towards the approaching visitors.

Finally I heard the door opening down below, followed by Mary Petrie crying out.

'Simon!' she exclaimed. 'Steve! Philip! How nice of you to come!'

In feigned surprise I looked round, expecting to see three faces gazing up at me. Instead, they were lost from view, presumably gathered in a cluster around the doorway.

There arose a babble of excited voices, and then I heard Simon saying, 'He's on the roof, but he hasn't seen us yet.'

'Well, he'll be glad you've come,' replied Mary Petrie. 'He's been missing you all terribly.'

'What's he doing up there?' asked Steve.

'Oh, he's messing about pretending to measure the chimney. He'll be down in a minute.'

I heard a boot scuff the ground, and next thing Steve appeared with a big grin on his face.

'How's the weathercock?' he called.

'Fine!' I replied. 'Never been wrong yet!'

'That's good! Are you going to come down and say hello then?'

His tone of voice wasn't at all like the abrupt and impatient Steve Treacle I was used to. Instead it was what I could only describe as 'more than friendly'. He was still smiling, and for some reason this made me feel quite vulnerable up there on the roof.

'I can't get down!' I heard myself say.

'Oh dear!' he replied. 'Wait there and I'll get help!'

Moments later the others had arrived on the scene, offering words of comfort. I couldn't see Philip, but I could hear someone scrabbling up the tin walls, and in a moment his head appeared quite close to me.

'Don't worry,' he said. 'You'll soon be safe.'

The next few minutes were a blur of helping hands and guiding voices. In an utterly helpless state I was manoeuvred downwards until eventually I stood swaying on solid ground.

'There, there,' said Simon, putting his arm around my shoulder.

'Thanks,' I mumbled. 'I thought I was going to be there for the night.'

'You're alright now, though, aren't you?'

'Oh yes. Never better.'

My weak attempt to make light of the matter didn't appear to register with my rescuers. Instead, they all stood round enquiring how I felt and asking if I'd like to lie down for a while. It occurred to me that because of this incident I was now indebted to the three of them, and my actual feeling was one not of relief, but of irritation. To tell them would have been churlish, however, so after I'd recovered sufficiently I invited them into the house.

This was the first time that Simon, Steve and Philip had sat down at my table together, yet I couldn't help noticing how relaxed they all seemed as a group. It was almost as if they'd spent many days and nights doing nothing but talking and getting to know one another. This I could imagine Simon doing quite easily, but I wouldn't have expected it of Philip. Nevertheless, there he was in the thick of the conversation, speaking with great confidence to Mary Petrie. For her part she appeared to find our three guests quite fascinating. I'd assumed she would do her disappearing act up the stairs as soon as we got inside, but instead she joined us in the kitchen and started asking all sorts of questions.

'So,' she began. 'What brings you back to these parts then?'

'I suppose we're on a mission really,' replied Philip.

'A mission?'

'Yes,' he said. 'We have an important task ahead of us.'

'Don't tell me you've come to fix the chimney?'

'Not primarily, no.'

Philip glanced at Steve, who was now gazing intently in my direction.

'Is that why you were on the roof?' he asked.

'Sort of,' I answered. 'Just having a look really. We think the chimney needs lengthening.'

'I see.'

'I suppose you wouldn't know how to do it, would you?'

I asked the question as casually as possible, because I didn't want Steve to think I was dependent on him in any way. There was a long pause before he replied, during which I realized he had ceased his habit of continually drumming on the table top.

Instead he sat calm and still in the place opposite mine, with his hands resting before him. Then, at last, he spoke.

'I can't do it for you,' he said. 'I can only show you how.'

Simon and Philip were seated each side of him, looking

as though they approved of every word. Their eyes were on me, and I felt like I was being urged to accept some generous yet unspecified offer. At the same time I saw that Mary Petrie was regarding our visitors with a bemused expression.

'Oh well,' I said. 'Good job I'm a fast learner.'

Steve nodded his head solemnly.

'Do you have any spare pieces of tin on the premises?' asked Philip.

'No, sorry, I don't.'

He looked genuinely surprised. 'What, none at all?'

'No.'

'But what if a stranger came by and asked for some?' said Simon. 'What would you do then?'

'Don't know,' I replied.

'Has it never happened?'

'No, actually, it hasn't!'

Mary Petrie must have realized that this line of talk was beginning to nettle me, because she suddenly rose from her seat and said, 'I don't suppose any of you have eaten?'

'Not for some hours,' said Steve.

'Alright,' she announced. 'I'll prepare something.'

'You're so kind,' remarked Simon. 'Thank you.'

The previous atmosphere of conviviality quickly returned to the table, and for the time being they stopped interrogating me about whether I had any spare pieces of tin. Then I remembered a question of my own.

'By the way, Simon,' I said. 'How did you get along when it came to putting your house back together again?'

This caused all three of them to look at each other and smile. It seemed my enquiry had triggered off some happy collective memory.

'Oh, quite a disaster really,' Simon replied. 'None of the parts would fit properly.'

'My fault, of course,' added Steve. 'We couldn't tell the roof from the walls, the back from the front, or anything. It was like a pig's ear when we'd finished.'

He had now turned slightly pink and sat there with a bashful grin on his face, as if joyfully recalling some past foolishness. This was a complete change from the assertive confidence he'd shown a few moments earlier, and I was at a loss to explain why. Meanwhile, the other two appeared equally delighted that things had gone so wrong with Simon's house.

They exchanged further smiles, then Philip said, 'Fortunately for us, Michael Hawkins had the solution.'

A murmur of assent arose from his companions, and out of the corner of my eye I saw Mary Petrie glance at me.

'Really?' I managed to say.

'Oh yes,' declared Simon in an eager voice. 'Michael built his own house of tin, you see, so he knew what had to be done. With his guidance we simply took mine to pieces and made it whole again.'

'That was lucky,' I said.

'Oh, it was more than luck,' said Steve. 'There's so much that Michael has learned, because he's lived out there so long. He's studied the lie of the land, and he knows which way the wind blows, and when the sun will rise and set. He showed us the best place to build our houses.'

'So that's where you've all moved to, is it?'

'Us and many others.'

'Just to be near this Michael Hawkins?'

'Yes,' he said. 'And we'd like you to join us.'

'Me?'

'Well, both of you really.' Steve now included Mary

Petrie in his gaze. 'Michael has requested it especially.'

    'Well, why didn't he come and ask us himself?'

    'Because he's far too busy.'

    'What with?'

    'He's creating a canyon for us all to live in.'

13

All at once I felt as if someone had pulled a hidden lever and caused a trapdoor to open beneath me. Only Mary Petrie knew of my abandoned desire to live in a canyon, and I trusted her with the secret. Yet here was this upstart, this Michael Hawkins, taunting me from beyond the horizon by means of his three messengers. What, I asked myself, was so special about him that they flocked to be at his side? After all, he only dwelt in a house of tin, same as I did. Just because he'd learnt a trick or two about predicting the weather, and knew how to assemble a few composite parts, they spoke of him in hushed tones as if he held some great gift for them. Now, I gathered, his boundless abilities even encompassed the creation of a canyon!

'What, on his own?' I asked.

'Oh, no,' replied Steve. 'It's going to need many hands to undertake such a work.'

'That's what I'd have thought.'

'So you'll come will you?' he asked.

'Well, I—'

'Michael can achieve great things with friends like us to

help him!' declared Simon, before I could even speak. 'There's a space already set aside for your house, if you're interested, and many people are looking forward to meeting you.'

While all this talk was going on, Mary Petrie had remained silent. Even so, I knew from the occasional looks she cast in my direction that she was listening to every word. Now, as Simon, Steve and Philip sat and waited like supplicants for an answer, she spoke directly to me.

'Won't it be a bit of a palaver moving everything?' she asked.

That was all she said, but I sensed instantly that the verdict had already been reached.

As I looked at her pictures on the walls, her china in the kitchen, and her carefully arranged vases of dried grass, I realized I would never get her to move an inch, let alone to some vague destination in an incomplete canyon.

She then offered refreshments to our guests, while I explained that we had to decline their invitation for reasons they would surely understand. Steve answered that he spoke for all in saying how disappointed he was that we wouldn't be coming. Nonetheless, he said, it was our decision, and if we ever changed our minds we only had to head west and we would easily find the way.

They left some time later, each of them calling their goodbyes to Mary Petrie, who had by now retired upstairs for the evening.

I watched as they set off into the darkness, and pondered whether I should have offered beds for the night instead of just allowing them to leave. In truth, however, I knew it was quite unnecessary. All they wanted to do was hurry back into the presence of Michael Hawkins, even though they were returning empty-handed.

They clearly believed he was central to their existence.

Well, they were welcome to him as far as I was concerned! I had no intention of living in thrall to someone else, even if he was building a canyon! And, indeed, the more I thought about that, the more absurd it sounded. Who did he think he was, exactly, setting himself such a task?

Clearly, it couldn't be done.

'He would need hundreds, maybe thousands, of people,' I explained to Mary Petrie a few days later. 'All properly directed, and sharing the same sense of purpose. How's he going to do that? It's impossible.'

'Really?' she said.

'Oh yes,' I replied. 'There's a limit to what any one man can achieve, and I'm afraid our friend Michael Hawkins has overreached himself.'

'You sure about that?'

'Certain.'

To my surprise, Mary Petrie rose to her feet and walked to the door.

'Well,' she announced. 'I've decided I was wrong.'

'Wrong?' I asked. 'How do you mean?'

'I was wrong to discourage you,' she answered. 'You'll have to go to this canyon after all.'

'But I thought you didn't want to move,' I said. 'That was why I sent Steve and the others away.'

'No, I don't want to move, I'm quite settled here. That doesn't mean you can't go and have a look, though.'

'Oh, it's alright. I'm not really interested.'

'So how come you keep going on about it day and night?'

'I didn't know I did.'

'Well you do!' she snapped. 'As a matter of fact, you've spoken of nothing else since those three left! You even talk

about it in your sleep, and if you don't know the reason
I'll tell you! It's because you once had great aspirations!
Remember? You were going to search the world for an
immense red canyon, remote and empty, where you'd live
in a house built entirely from tin. You told me this in all
its detail. No other life would do, you said, yet somehow
you wound up stuck on a flat and featureless plain! Now
you've heard about a man creating the very place you were
talking about, and as long as you know it's there you'll
never be satisfied!'

Suddenly Mary Petrie threw open the door. 'Go on!' she
ordered. 'Go and see it for yourself!'

*   *   *

As I departed she seized the hammer and began using it to
beat a saucepan flat. I could still hear the metallic blows
when I was half a mile away. At this distance they reminded
me of the chimes from Simon Painter's bell, but they had
none of the forlorn tones that had been so familiar a year
ago. Instead they clanged out a simple, strident message: 'I
am going to fix the chimney whether you like it or not!'

I thought about Mary Petrie while I headed west, and
remembered how helpless she'd seemed when she first
arrived. She'd brought with her a world that revolved
around a trunk, a mirror and a vanity case, and knew nothing about living in a tin house. The sound of that hammer,
fading away behind me, was evidence that she had since
become fully conversant with the subject.

The wind was blowing hard that day, and sent ripples of
sand scurrying across the plain. It was not enough, though,

to disturb the many trails of footprints I encountered. Throughout my journey I came upon them, all heading resolutely west. I passed the places where Simon, Steve and Philip had once lived, and then continued into the hinterland, not knowing quite what to expect.

By now some of the trails had merged to form more obvious routes, and I noticed that once they'd joined together like this they never separated again. After I'd been going for some while I began to yearn for the sight of a stray set of footprints wandering off to the left or to the right, choosing their own direction rather than merely following the crowd. None appeared.

All the same, I had to admit I found the excursion fairly interesting. Several times I stopped to examine the points where various trails converged, and on each occasion tried to work out if people were travelling alone or in groups, and even whether they were carrying loads.

Those who were, I guessed, were the ones with the heavier tread.

It was now approaching early evening. I remembered something about Simon taking five hours to get to Michael Hawkins's place. That being so, I reckoned I should be in the vicinity by now, and therefore I stopped and peered around me. The day had been wild and blustery, with a grey sky that was already beginning to darken in the north. To the west, however, some light persisted, and as I stood looking I saw the dull and unmistakeable glint of a house of tin.

At the same instant my eye was caught by a similar glint slightly to the left of the first. Suspecting that maybe my sight was playing tricks on me in the failing conditions, I blinked once or twice. When I tried again I saw yet another glimmer, somewhat further away. Now I was certain. There, about a mile distant, stood at least three houses, maybe more, all built from tin. In the acute and final rays of daylight I attempted to count them. This time I made it five, but then an additional gleam emerged from the dimness, so that was six.

'I will if you will,' said a voice behind me.

Startled, I turned quickly to see a man advancing from the way I'd just come. He was carrying a bag and had addressed me in a very familiar tone, even though I'd never seen him before.

'Pardon?' I asked.

'I will if you will,' he repeated.

'Will what?'

'You know,' he said. 'Complete the journey. Take the final step, as it were. I'm about to do the same thing.'

'Oh, I see.'

'Savouring the moment, were you?'

'Sort of.'

'Thought so. The name's Patrick Pybus, by the way. I've been following you for the last hour and I noticed you've been moving very slowly. You kept stopping all the time and studying footprints. That's how I caught you up so easily. Then you stood here for another five minutes without moving at all.'

'Yes,' I said. 'Well, I was just looking at all this lot.'

I pointed in the direction of the tin houses and realized there was now nothing to see, the dusk having enveloped the plain. Even so, Patrick Pybus seemed to understand perfectly what I was talking about.

'Marvellous, isn't it?!' he exclaimed. 'The years I've wanted to do this, and now I'm finally here! What a life! I can't wait to sit by the stove late at night, listening to the wind as it plays under the eaves, the four walls creaking and groaning! Here, I've got something to show you.'

He reached into his bag and produced a large piece of paper, folded, which he carefully opened out for me. I peered at it in the gloom and saw a drawing of a house of tin. This had been done in a very correct manner, with proper measurements and so forth, and bore a strong resemblance to my own house. On closer examination, however, I decided it was more like Simon Painter's.

'Very nice,' I said. 'Is this where you're going to live?'

'When it's built, yes,' he replied.

'Well, shouldn't you be carrying some tin along with you?'

'I've got some friends coming along behind,' he said. 'They're bringing the tin with them.'

'Then they'll be going back, will they?'

'No, they'll be staying.'

'But what about their own tin?' I asked.

'Their own tin?'

'Yes,' I said. 'If they're bringing the tin for your house, they won't be able to bring their own as well, will they?'

'Oh no,' he said. 'It's not like that. We're going to be sharing.'

'Sharing? What, all in one house?'

'Yes, of course. Why not?'

'Well . . .' I began, but then trailed off. One look at Patrick Pybus told me it would be futile trying to explain the finer points of living in a house of tin. He was simply too enthusiastic to understand that primarily you needed to be alone, and miles from the next person. Maybe in time he would learn this, and certainly there was enough room on this vast and empty plain for any amount of tin houses. Meanwhile, I just couldn't bring myself to blunt his fervour.

'Well, good luck,' I said.

'Same to you,' he replied. 'Shall we press on then?'

'No, you go ahead if you like. I think I'll stay here a bit longer.'

'Right you are,' he said. 'See you.'

I watched Patrick Pybus disappear along the trail, then followed behind at a more leisurely pace, not being in quite such a hurry as him. To tell the truth, I'd been somewhat alarmed by the sight of all those tin houses. I had a feeling that the ones I'd counted were only the first of many, judging by the amount of footprints coming in this direction. True, there was a possibility that the numerous travellers we'd observed over the past year had been heading for a wide and varied set of destinations. In reality, though, I suspected they were all gravitating towards the same place. This made me wonder how I was going to cope when I got there. I was used to living in isolation with only Mary Petrie for company. The prospect of all those people, waiting less than a mile away, was frankly quite daunting, and as a result I took my time.

Another question was where I was going to spend the night. I had no doubt that Simon, Steve and Philip would all make me quite welcome, but first I had to find one of their houses. I was now drawing near to the half dozen or so I'd seen earlier, but I had no idea whether any of them belonged to my friends. In former days I'd always known whose place I was approaching simply because of its location. Simon lived to the west of me, for example, while Steve lived west-north-west of him. Here, where the houses all stood together, it was difficult to tell them apart. Admittedly they varied slightly, some being higher than others, or having different gable ends. Essentially, however, they were all the same. Each was built entirely from tin.

The moon had now begun to make fitful appearances

amongst the clouds, and as my eyes grew accustomed to its pale light I saw many rooftops ahead. Shortly afterwards I was passing between the first of the houses, and I noticed that the shutters were all firmly closed, as were the doors. I found it pleasing to think that this tradition was being maintained in what was basically a new settlement. Up until now I'd assumed that these newcomers would be the types who'd want to keep their shutters thrown open whatever the weather. Instead, it seemed, they had more sense. Already this evening, accumulations of sand had begun to drift against the tin walls, but it looked unlikely that any was going to enter these dwellings. I paused next to one of them and listened. Inside, I could hear the sound of muffled conversation. Also, somebody singing. I moved on.

There was no fixed distance between the houses, nor did they appear to have been laid out in any uniform pattern. Instead there were rows heading off in all directions, higgledy-piggledy, as if each had been added one after another. I recalled Steve's remark about Michael Hawkins having shown them where to build their houses, and I tried to work out the logic of the arrangement. The only thing I could see for sure was that they were all sited very close together, but for the moment I had no idea why.

The trouble with wandering along in the dark like this was that it was easy to forget which way I'd come. I knew I'd turned right at a house with four front shutters and two at the sides, and had then walked past one with a markedly angled roof. Yet when I returned a short distance to check my bearings, I couldn't find either of them. Continuing back a little further, I discovered a side-junction I hadn't noticed before. I followed it round.

Then, somewhere away to my left, I heard the faint clanging of a bell. It was a sound I'd recognize anywhere, and soon I was standing outside Simon Painter's house. There was no captive balloon hoisted in the air above it, nor was there a flagpole on the roof. Nevertheless, I knew I had the right place. The bell hung on a bracket beside the door, swaying gently in the breeze and chiming from time to time. I was about to make myself known when I heard a peal of laughter within. It came from several voices, one of which I knew to be Simon's. The rest belonged to women. I waited and heard Simon say something else, then more laughter followed.

It certainly sounded as if they were having a good time in there, and I was reluctant to interrupt. Just then, however, the door opened and a smiling young woman emerged. When she noticed me standing there, partially hidden by shadows, she appeared not at all surprised.

'Simon!' she called into the house. 'We've got a visitor!'

'Come in!' I heard him cry. 'Come in! Whoever it is!'

Apparently the young woman was just heading off somewhere. She smiled and held the door for me.

'Thanks,' I managed.

'That's OK,' she replied, slipping away through the darkness. I hesitated for a few more seconds, then stepped over the threshold.

14

As I entered, Simon was half-rising from behind a table, around which sat four women and another man.

'Hello!' he boomed. 'You decided to join us after all!'

'Yes, well,' I replied. 'I thought I'd come and have a look anyway.'

'Good! Good! Michael will be so pleased to see you!'

There then followed a swirl of greetings, handshakes and introductions as I met the rest of the group, all of whom apparently knew I was an ex-neighbour of Simon's. Not being used to dealing with so many people at once, I found their names tended to go straight in one ear and out the other. Nonetheless, they treated me like a long lost friend. Soon I had a drink in my hand and a place of honour at the table. Simon immediately told the story of how his house had been dismantled while he was away, and how I'd gone over to help him out. He described his despair at seeing the pieces of tin all stacked up on top of each other, his former existence thereby reduced to a meaningless puzzle. Inevitably, of course, we had to listen to the bit at the end where Michael Hawkins came along and put everything right again. It quickly became clear that Simon was an established raconteur amongst his new-found circle of friends, and I was quietly impressed by the way they listened enthralled to every word he said. All the same, I was slightly baffled by his earlier comment that Michael would be so pleased to see me, as though this had some extra special significance. If he'd said, '*I'm* so pleased to see you', or even '*Steve* will be so pleased to see you', I could have understood the remark perfectly. Instead, it seemed only to matter what this Michael Hawkins thought, and I wondered why Simon should abase himself in such a manner. Still, there was no cause to dwell on these questions right now. The present company was most acceptable and I had nothing to complain about. Quite the opposite actually. While Simon was talking, I began to notice I was getting a good deal of attention from one of the women. Several times she cast meaningful glances in my direction, and she smiled at all the parts of the story that involved me. I had a feeling she was called Jane, which was one of the names that had been bandied around during the introductions, but I couldn't be sure. For the moment I decided I would just have to pretend I knew her name, and see how things went. Judging by the looks she gave me, the prospects were certainly promising.

In the meantime, Simon's tale was coming to an end.

'These days we can build a house of tin with our eyes shut,' he concluded. 'But, of course, it helps if we keep them open!'

There followed a gale of laughter from his listeners, and it struck me that Simon's gift as a storyteller was in marked contrast to the streams of enquiry which had characterized his past conversations. I thought back to those dreary afternoons when he'd questioned me on whether I'd seen Steve or heard from Philip, and I decided that the new Simon was a great improvement. If only he would stop going on about Michael Hawkins! He was at it again a few minutes later when the woman who'd let me in returned.

'Michael could be coming to visit us tomorrow,' she announced. 'I've just seen Philip and he says there's a strong probability.'

As she spoke her eyes were sparkling, and in the same instant I felt a stir of anticipation pass round the table.

'Oh that's marvellous,' said Simon. 'Did he tell you when, exactly?'

'No, it's not definite yet,' replied the woman. 'It depends on how well the canyon is going.'

'Of course,' he uttered, almost inaudibly. 'I understand.'

'How is Philip?' I asked, but Simon hardly seemed to hear.

'Michael's work never ceases!' he said. 'Day after day he conducts operations in that canyon! It's already deeper and wider than any of us could have ever imagined, yet still he goes on. We implore him to rest, and to come and take refreshment in our houses. Instead he chooses to work. Those of us who help him do all we can to lessen his burden, but in the end only he can decide when to stop. This news from Philip is most encouraging!'

The new woman came to join us at the table, which meant we each had to move round a little bit. She was introduced as Sarah, and soon she was telling everyone the latest tidings about Michael Hawkins and his possible forthcoming visit. Meanwhile, I again found myself under the gaze of the other woman, the one who'd been paying me all the attention earlier. Beside her sat the only man present apart from Simon and I. He was leaning back in his seat, peering intently at the roof as though carrying out a thorough examination. Eventually the talk subsided into a sort of reverent hush, and at last he broke his silence.

'Listen to that,' he said, his eyes still raised to the roof. 'Can you hear it?'

The only sound was the wind playing beneath the eaves. It was something I'd heard on a thousand or more occasions, in my own part of the plain, yet now I was being urged to listen to it as if for the first time in my life.

'Ah yes,' I replied. 'The wind.'

'Isn't it wonderful?' asked Sarah, in an exultant voice.

As we all sat there with our heads tilted slightly to one side, it occurred to me that this was probably one of Michael Hawkins's ideas too. Fortunately, it didn't go on very long, and I was pleasantly surprised when my admirer suddenly glanced across at me and spoke.

'Quite a crowd we've got here,' she remarked. 'Why don't you come along and have a look at my house?'

'Well,' I said. 'I'd like to, but . . . er . . . would that be alright with you, Simon?'

'By all means,' he replied, with a friendly shrug. 'Go wherever you're most comfortable.'

'I haven't seen Steve and Philip yet,' I pointed out.

'Don't worry on that score,' he said. 'There's plenty of time!'

'Shall we go now then?' said the woman.

*　　*　　*

We went out into the darkness, and a moment later she took me by the hand.

'It's hard finding your way when you first get here,'

she explained. 'But it's quite simple once you're used to it.'

Certainly I would have been lost without her to guide me. There was no one else about, and everywhere we turned there were houses of tin, all with their shutters closed for the evening. They were mostly silent, the hour now being late, but from within some of them we heard soft murmurings.

'Did you say your name was Jane?' I asked.

'Yes,' she replied. 'Jane Day.'

'How long have you been here?'

'Oh, I'm a fairly recent arrival. Got swept along with the others.'

'And do you intend to stay here for a bit?'

'Of course!' she said. 'I want to find out all there is about living in a house of tin! I expect you know a lot more on the subject than most people, don't you?'

'I suppose I do, yes.'

'Well, if there's anything you want to teach me, I'll be happy to learn!'

As we walked I managed once or twice to steal a glance at her in the moonlight. At the same time I tried to work out what it was that appealed to me so much. In truth, I had to admit that her attractions were no greater than those of Mary Petrie. They were just different, that was all.

After a while we began heading towards a particular building, rather than just wandering along. I peered ahead and saw that it was a fairly typical tin house, with no unusual features.

'Is this it?' I enquired.

'Yes,' she said. 'What do you think?'

'Looks fine to me.'

'Have you felt the walls?'

'No.'

She smiled. 'Well, go on then.'

I placed my hand upon the corrugations, and at once recognized the coldness of the metal. It was just the same as the walls of my own tin dwelling all those miles away. For some reason this caused a surge of guilt to rise up inside me, and I had to struggle for several moments to overcome it.

'Shall we go in?' I suggested.

The first thing I noticed when we entered was that the inside was a precise replica of Simon's house. There was a table in the kitchen, with four or five chairs placed around it, and in the corner a stove glowed brightly. Even the chimney went out through the roof exactly where Simon's did. On top of the stove was a pot of coffee.

'Ah, good,' said Jane. 'Alison must be back.'

'Who's Alison?' I asked.

Some feet could be heard on the stairs, and a few seconds later a woman appeared. I knew her immediately. She was one of the three I'd encountered when I went to collect the basket from Simon's old place.

'Oh, it's you,' she said when she saw me. 'I heard you might be coming.'

'Have you two met each other before then?' asked Jane.

'Just once,' came the reply.

I remembered this Alison being quite unfriendly on the occasion of our first meeting. Hostile even. Something told me that she was a permanent resident here, and all at once I realized I wouldn't be spending the night alone with Jane. For her part, she appeared totally oblivious to the cool manner in which Alison was regarding me from the stairway.

'He's come to see our house of tin,' she explained.

'Has he?' said Alison. 'How nice for us.'

'I can go back to Simon's if you like,' I said.

'No, it's alright,' she replied, in a resigned tone. 'Now you're here you might as well make yourself at home.'

It turned out that Jane really had invited me back just to talk about tin houses. For the next hour she quizzed me with such questions as when was the best time to open or close the shutters, and what strength of wind would make the walls creak and groan. As we talked I got the strong impression that she already knew most of the answers, but that she was keen to embrace the subject even further. Oddly enough, though, the more she enthused about it the less interested I became. As a matter of fact I found her eagerness quite exhausting, and was consequently relieved when at last Alison intervened.

'Don't you think that's enough for one night?' she said. 'Our guest must be getting tired.'

'Oh, I do apologize!' Jane exclaimed, jumping to her feet. 'You must think me very rude.'

'No, no,' I replied. 'I've found the whole evening most fascinating.'

She then began rushing round preparing somewhere for me to sleep. This hadn't been exactly what I'd envisaged when accepting her invitation, but I was now so tired that I no longer cared. Ten minutes later I was installed in a camp-bed on the ground floor, and the women had made their way upstairs. In many respects it was just like being in my own house on one of those rare nights when, for undisclosed reasons, Mary Petrie would banish me from the upper storey. I thought of her as I lay listening to muted footsteps moving around on the floor above, and then I dozed off to sleep.

Sometime in the dead of night I was woken by the sound of the door opening and people coming in. They weren't noisy or intrusive, and had soon dispersed to various parts of the house, except for one who remained downstairs. I heard bedding being unrolled in the darkness, so I thought it might be polite to let him or her know that I was there. Whoever it was seemed to be fumbling around quite a lot, as if unacquainted with the layout of the place, and this provided my opportunity to speak.

'Do you need help with that?' I asked quietly.

The other person gasped with surprise, then answered, 'No, I'm fine thanks.'

'Is that Patrick Pybus?'

'Yes,' he said. 'Is that you I met on the way here?'

'Yes it is. How did you get on this evening?'

'Very well indeed, thanks. I appear to have landed right on my feet. I've already come across two of your friends, Steve Treacle and Philip Sibling, and they arranged for me to stay here tonight.' He lowered his voice. 'The girls are all very friendly aren't they?'

'Most of the time, yes,' I said. 'What are Steve and Philip up to?'

'They've been helping Michael Hawkins with the canyon. I'm going to see it tomorrow. Have you met him yet?'

'No, I haven't had the pleasure.'

'Nor me, but I'm really looking forward to it. They say he's doing some marvellous work out there, and can turn his hand to any task. Not that you need telling, of course. You're already well-versed in his achievements.'

Patrick had now adopted the hushed tones I'd become used to when people spoke about Michael Hawkins. There was an expectant pause as his words sunk in.

'Me?' I said, at last.

'Yes,' he replied. 'After all, it was Michael who built your house, wasn't it?'

15

Patrick spoke the words as though they were a truth set in stone.

'Who told you that?' I asked.

'Several people,' he said. 'Didn't you know?'

'No, I didn't.'

'Well, the story is that Michael started constructing it long ago when he was still seeking his way here. Tin was plentiful in those days, so he came onto the plain and set to work raising his house. Not until he'd finished did he realize the mistake he'd made.'

'Which was?'

'He'd built it on sand, and therefore he had to abandon it and start again somewhere else.'

I lay in the darkness and listened with mounting dismay. After all, this was my house of tin we were talking about! Admittedly, I'd discovered it standing empty and deserted in the middle of the plain, but never had I questioned how it came to exist. As far as I was concerned it was just there for the taking, so I'd moved in and made it my home. If this story was correct, then I was a usurper.

'Well, why has it never fallen down?' I asked. 'Answer me that.'

'I can't,' replied Patrick. 'I'm just telling you what the others told me. Maybe your house will last for many years. It should do if Michael built it. Then again, he wouldn't have forsaken it for no reason, would he? It could collapse next week for all we know.'

'That seems unlikely.'

'Well, it doesn't matter anyway. You're here now, so you'll be quite safe.'

'But aren't these houses built on sand as well?'

'No, not according to Steve and Philip. Apparently Michael dug down and found clay underneath.'

'I see.'

'Reassuring to know you're on solid ground, isn't it?'

'Suppose so.'

'Goodnight, then.'

'Night.'

Judging from the sounds he made, Patrick Pybus fell asleep more or less the moment his head touched the pillow. It took me a little longer.

*   *   *

The dominant news next morning was that Michael Hawkins's long-awaited visit would have to be postponed yet again. From what I could gather, there were so many volunteers helping him with his canyon that he was reluctant to leave them unsupervised. I learnt this as I sat at breakfast with Jane, Alison and Patrick, as well as two other women who'd come in during the night. These I recognized as

Alison's travelling companions. By the time I awoke, Jane had already been out on an early morning errand.

'I saw Steve Treacle,' she explained. 'He told me Michael will be staying in the canyon for another day at least.'

'How far away is it?' I asked.

'About two miles,' she said.

'Well, doesn't he go home in the evenings?'

'Oh no. He always stays with his helpers.'

It turned out that the canyon was now so immense it wasn't deemed worthwhile for these volunteers to return to their houses each night. Instead they sheltered under tarpaulins and remained on site for three or four days at a time. When eventually they did come back, they were immediately replaced by fresh recruits.

'Our turn next!' said Jane. 'I can't wait to get out there and lend a hand.'

Alison, I noticed, didn't look quite so enthusiastic.

'Well, I wish Michael would inform us when he's changing his arrangements,' she sighed. 'He's let us down like this before.'

'He is very busy, you know,' Jane pointed out.

'Yes,' replied Alison. 'I am aware of that.'

Despite her initial hostility, I found I actually preferred Alison to the rest of them. She had none of the sweetness and light that exuded from all the others, and which I thought rather tedious. On the contrary, she struck me as coming very much from the Mary Petrie sort of mould, and I had a feeling we would probably get on alright together in the end.

'Steve says he'd like to take you to the canyon today if you're interested,' said Jane, turning to me. 'He'll be here to collect you this morning.'

Before he arrived I decided to go outside for a look

around in broad daylight. Patrick Pybus accompanied me. Having always been accustomed to the sight of lone structures in remote locations, I found it most peculiar seeing all those houses in close proximity to one another. I gazed along winding passageways with tin walls no more than an arm's length apart. These widened out in some places to create streets and thoroughfares. Even so, there were very few people out and about.

'They tend to spend a lot of time indoors,' said Patrick. 'Especially if they've been helping with the canyon for a few days. It can be quite tiring work, so I've heard.'

'You seem to have learnt a great deal,' I remarked. 'Considering you only got here a few hours ago.'

'Well,' he replied. 'I thought I'd better find out about everything since I'm planning to live in these parts.'

'You've definitely decided then, have you?'

'Oh, without question. Philip's going to show me the proposed site for my house today. They've all been most welcoming.'

'Yes, I've noticed.'

Patrick gave me a knowing look. 'It's you they're keenest to have here, though.'

'Is it?' I asked, slightly surprised.

'Certainly,' he said. 'Everyone's delighted you've finally turned up. It means a lot to them, you being one of the pioneers, so to speak.'

This was confirmed some minutes later when Steve Treacle arrived, attended by an entourage of fresh-faced followers. Suddenly there was a great kerfuffle, and they emerged from a nearby avenue. I could see instantly that Steve had considerable standing amongst these people, because as he approached me they held back a little.

This, I assumed, was out of respect for the pair of us.

'So you've come!' he declared, smiling and offering his hand. 'Michael will be so pleased.'

I ignored the latter comment, and instead greeted Steve and enquired about his health and suchlike. Then I explained the purpose of my visit. 'I want to see this canyon I've heard so much about.'

'And so you shall,' Steve replied. 'These are all the new helpers going there today.'

He motioned to those behind him, and they came forward at last, surrounding me and asking all sorts of questions about my life in a house of tin. I was practically mobbed, such was their zeal. The clamour of voices caused several doors to open in the adjacent dwellings, from where numerous onlookers watched the scene with interest. Soon we were joined by Alison, Jane and the rest of them, and Steve suggested we should depart immediately for the canyon.

Never before had I encountered such an eager stream of people. They seemed to flow in from all directions, and as we progressed through this burgeoning city I realized for the first time just how many travellers had crossed the plain to get here. Steve and I were at the head of a column at least a hundred strong, all talking to one another in excited, joyful voices. The exception was Alison. She walked along in comparative silence and only appeared to speak when someone addressed her. I'd learnt since my arrival that her full name was Alison Hopewell, but each time I saw her I was again reminded of Mary Petrie, whom I'd left so far behind. It was hard to believe that we had only parted yesterday. Here, in my place at the forefront of the surging crowd, it felt like an age ago.

Eventually the buildings began to peter out slightly, with empty spaces lying between them. At one such gap Philip Sibling was waiting to show Patrick where he and his friends might like to build their new home. We paused to let the main party move ahead, and then went over to have a look at the suggested site. Philip welcomed me and said he was glad I'd come, and that I would probably find all this most interesting.

'It's a good prime position here,' he told Patrick. 'One of the nearest there is to the canyon. We would recommend you built your house facing west, of course, then you'll catch a glimpse of the sunset.'

'Perfect,' remarked Patrick, measuring out the ground in long, even paces. 'Just perfect.'

'Don't mind me asking,' I said. 'But won't it be a bit cramped with all the buildings jammed so close together? Looks to me like there'll hardly be enough room between them.'

'These sites were laid out by Michael himself,' said Steve. 'There is actually sufficient space here for an entire house.'

'We have a similar plot set aside for you,' added Philip. 'Or, of course, you could have the first option on this one, if you preferred.'

At these words an expression of deep disappointment crossed Patrick's face.

'No, no,' I said. 'Let Patrick have it. I insist.'

'Well, if you're sure . . .'

'Yes, that's alright.'

'Thank you,' said Patrick.

When I again glanced at Steve, I noticed he was regarding me with a rather stern visage.

'Michael does know what he's talking about,' he announced.

'So I gather,' I replied. 'I've heard all about my house being built on sand.'

'Precisely,' said Steve. 'This settlement has been constructed under his specific guidance, and we don't question any of the decisions.'

'That sounds fair enough to me,' I said. 'Who am I to argue?'

Steve glared at me for a few moments more before giving me a curt nod.

'Very well,' he managed, in a firm but polite tone. 'Shall we go on?'

I said a hasty goodbye to Philip and Patrick, and then set off after Steve, who had already marched away. I caught up with him just as he passed between the last of the houses. Shortly after that we emerged once more onto the open plain, where I was relieved to find Alison waiting for us. Steve hadn't spoken for the last minute, so it was pleasant to have her company as well.

'What did you think of the site?' she asked.

'Very good,' I replied. 'Almost a home from home.'

'Should be just right for Patrick then.'

There was a clearly marked trail ahead, on which I could see remote figures moving. The volunteers for the canyon had now become strung out in a long line, many walking in single file, others travelling in pairs, and they never wavered from their steady course. I cast an eye along this determined procession, and then turned my gaze to the wide sweep of plain. Away to our right, about a mile distant, I noticed a house standing quite alone. I knew by its dull gleam that it was built from tin, and it also appeared to be positioned on a piece of land higher than its immediate surroundings. This made it look somehow elevated, as though set aside for some exalted person. I didn't bother to ask who lived there.

'How's Mary Petrie?' asked Steve, breaking his silence in an obvious attempt to resume normal relations.

'Fine,' I replied. 'It was on her insistence that I came, to tell the truth.'

'So she'll be joining us eventually, will she?'

'Well, I don't know about that,' I said. 'She's very fixed in her ways, you know.'

'And you're not, I suppose?'

'Of course I'm not. No one's more open to change than me.'

'Oh come, come,' he said. 'Surely you don't expect me to believe that. You're the only one who refused to move when the rest of us did.'

'That's because I was content where I was.'

'So what are you doing here then?'

'Answering your invitation, if you must know, but if I'd thought you were going to go on like this I wouldn't have bothered.'

'Will you two stop squabbling!' cried Alison suddenly. 'I thought you were supposed to be old friends!'

'We are,' said Steve. 'But—'

'Well, then!' she snapped. 'You've been continually pecking at each other since we set off, and it's got to stop! Whatever will Michael think?'

Personally, I didn't care what Michael thought, but all the same I was glad that Alison had intervened. The last thing I wanted was to fall out with Steve again, so I decided to change the subject.

'I'm really looking forward to seeing this canyon now,' I said. 'Do you reckon I should offer my assistance?'

'I think it would be most welcome,' said Steve. 'Especially as you're so handy with a shovel.'

It was a simple exchange of words, but more than enough to get us talking again, and soon I was having the canyon explained to me in detail. I learnt that Michael

Hawkins had begun the undertaking completely alone about a year ago. This was round about the time Simon Painter started making his visits. Other people journeyed in from different parts of the plain, and one by one they offered their help. Shortly afterwards Steve and Philip arrived, followed by yet more travellers. The numbers grew until eventually they had enough volunteers for operations to be organized on a larger scale. These were carried out under the auspices of Michael Hawkins, who seemed to have a genius for such matters. Apparently, it was merely a question of him suggesting that such and such a thing could be done, and within hours it would be achieved. By now the stage had been reached where a few hundred helpers were fulfilling the work of thousands.

As I listened to all this I began to wonder if some sort of trickery wasn't at hand, by which these people were being deluded. Indeed, I'd long suspected that Michael Hawkins had most likely discovered some natural fault, or fissure, out here on the plain, and then adapted it for his own use. The colourful account that Steve was giving me did nothing but confirm my scepticism. Ah yes, the canyon certainly existed. He'd not only seen it himself, but had actually taken part in its development. This, of course, was an indisputable fact, and the sight would no doubt be impressive. I was on my way to view a great work that offered purpose to numerous men and women. Nevertheless, I had a feeling it was being accomplished by hook and crook.

16

Steve was gradually quickening his pace.

At first I hardly noticed the difference and continued to match him stride for stride. Then I became aware that Alison was having to break into an occasional trot just to keep up with the pair of us. It struck me that he probably didn't even know he was doing it, and I was pleased to discover that in spite of some odd new traits, his inherent lack of patience remained intact. The slick smile with which he'd first greeted me had long since disappeared, suggesting that the original Steve Treacle wasn't far beneath the surface.

Eventually, though, the rate at which he was propelling us across the plain got too much for Alison.

'Can't we slow down a bit?' she demanded.

'Not really, no,' replied Steve.

'What's the big hurry?'

'I don't want to miss out on anything.'

'But the canyon's going to be there for ever!' she said. 'I'm sure it'll wait for you.'

Steve did his best to ease up a little, and we pressed on at a slightly slower speed than before. Ahead of us I could see that the first dozen or so volunteers had come to a halt, allowing those behind to catch up. For some reason, however, the leading bunch didn't appear to grow in size as the others joined it, but continued to number only about a dozen. All the rest were simply vanishing from sight. For a while I couldn't work out what was happening at all, and only when we drew closer did I realize that, having reached the edge of the canyon, they were now making their descent into it. Each individual would arrive at a certain point, pause for a moment, then drop out of view. The remaining group slowly dwindled, one by one, until all had followed.

Our small party still had a hundred yards to go, yet already I could see that the level of the plain had fallen away into nothingness. We carried on a bit further, and the far side of the canyon began to loom up into my line of vision. It was a sheer red wall, increasing in enormity as we got nearer. Finally we came to the precipice, where the sight that met us was truly unbelievable. I had never imagined it would be so deep and so wide, and I heard Alison gasp with astonishment. For several seconds I gazed down at the people, tiny as ants, moving around far below us. Then everything went hazy.

Next thing I knew I was sitting with my head between my legs.

'He'll be alright in a minute,' I heard Steve saying. 'He doesn't like heights, that's all.'

As I came to my senses again Alison put her arm round me.

'Well, well,' she remarked. 'I didn't think you'd be the type who fainted.'

'I'm not normally,' I said. 'But I don't think I can go down there.'

'Why don't you have another look and see if you feel better about it?'

She took me by the hand and led me back to the edge, where I took a deep breath before peering over. This time I managed to maintain some dignity by reminding myself that I was standing on firm ground.

'Isn't it amazing?' said Alison.

'Staggering, more like,' I replied.

How on earth had Michael Hawkins managed this? The canyon was of stupendous proportions, and I just failed to see how it could have been created by human toil, no matter how many helpers there were. As far as I could tell from this distance, all they had to work with was shovels. The latest batch of volunteers was still descending into these depths, by means of a series of ladders and earth ramps that formed a route down. Positioned at various places were rope-and-pulley hoists, on which laden buckets were being hauled up, emptied, and lowered again. At the bottom of the canyon were hundreds of workers, the men amongst them stripped to the waist, all digging or manoeuvring barrows along planks. Beyond them I could see an encampment of tarpaulins spread over poles. There were fires here, and people tending cooking pots, while others appeared to be resting.

After a while Steve announced that we really ought to get a move on, but by now I'd made my mind up.

'It's no good,' I said. 'I'll have to stay up here.'

'Don't you want to come down and help?' he asked.

'I do, yes, but I know I'll get into difficulty on those ladders, so there's no use even trying. Sorry and everything, but that's just how it is.'

Fortunately, Steve didn't press the issue. Instead he merely shrugged and said that I was missing out on a great opportunity. Alison seemed quite disappointed that I wasn't going any further, but at the same time insisted that she fully understood my position.

'Why don't you stay here and admire the view for a bit,' she suggested. 'You might feel more inclined to come down later.'

Although this was fairly unlikely, I decided that I would indeed stay where I was for a while. I felt a little empty as they started their descent, especially when Alison turned at the very rim of the canyon to give me a smile and a wave. Next moment she and Steve were gone, and I was alone once more.

One of the remarkable things about this canyon was the very redness of the earth. There was a lot of cloud today and the light was accordingly dim, but even so it was almost impossible not to be struck by the vivid spectacle. The sight of those towering walls was mesmerizing, and I must have passed a good hour gazing across the void. Presently, I heard voices coming from somewhere below me, and then two women appeared. Judging by their tired, slightly grimy appearance I guessed that they were helpers heading for home. When they saw me they smiled and asked how I was, before continuing on their way. The same thing happened a quarter of an hour later when a group of six men clambered out of the canyon. They, too, set off homeward after enquiring about my well-being. Another ten minutes went by. Next up was a young woman travelling on her own. She looked thoroughly exhausted as she completed the climb, but the moment she saw me her face brightened.

'Was it you who couldn't get down?' she asked.

'Yes,' I replied. ''Fraid so.'

'Oh, but you must try!' she declared. 'It would be most worthwhile if you could.'

'Why's that?'

'It's just wonderful there. Michael has organized every-thing perfectly, and the work is so rewarding!'

She had exactly the same kind of approach to life as Jane. Or possibly Sarah. Even her voice sounded similar to theirs. As she went on about how marvellous it was in the canyon, I couldn't help noticing how weary and dishevelled she looked. Nonetheless, she kept up her spirited appraisal of the place for some time, and I was impressed by her sense of conviction.

When she'd finished enthusing, I said, 'You'll be going home for a well-earned rest now, will you?'

'Yes,' she smiled. 'It's always so nice to get back after a few days' service.'

'Is that what it's called then?' I asked. 'Service?'

'That's Michael's word for it, yes. Well, bye then.'

'Bye,' I said.

This mass exodus of spent workers from the canyon began to acquire a certain fascination for me. I sat at the top for a couple of hours as various groups and individuals came by, all uttering some nicety before returning across the plain towards the city of tin. It was obvious from their step that every one of them was looking forward to getting back to the comfort of their own houses after several days under the tarpaulins.

I was engaged watching a jaded-looking couple wander away, hand in hand, when a man emerged travelling alone. He stood for some moments gazing into the canyon, then turned to me.

'Great view, isn't it?' he said.

'Yes,' I replied. 'But to tell the truth it's even more interesting watching the people go by.'

'A fellow after my own heart,' he announced. 'Certainly, we've got some fine men and women here.'

'I can believe that.'

'By the way, have you had anything to eat?'

'No, not for some hours,' I said. 'Expect I'll be given something back at Simon Painter's, though.'

'They're just making some supper in the camp, if you're interested.'

'Thanks, but the trouble is I can't get down.'

'Have you tried?'

'Er . . . no, I haven't, actually.'

'Well, why don't you?' he said. 'Who knows? You might succeed.'

I looked at this man and saw from the state of his clothes that he must have been working exceptionally hard. His hands were engrained with the red earth he'd had to shovel all day long, and he was probably keen to hasten home for a break. Yet despite all this he seemed most concerned that I should partake of the supper that was being cooked down below.

'I'm not very keen on ladders,' I explained.

'Well, they're all properly secured,' he said. 'I can assure you of that.'

'Oh, are they?'

'Yes, and the earth ramps are as safe as houses.'

There was something about the way he spoke that made me trust him unreservedly, as if I'd known him my whole life. All at once I felt that I might just be able to negotiate the route into the canyon, if someone came with me.

'I don't mind accompanying you,' said the man. 'If you'd like to have a go.'

'Alright,' I replied. 'I will.'

The first part of the descent was a short, steep ramp of earth leading to a platform about twelve feet below. I got down this section quite easily, and then found myself at the top of a long ladder. The man hopped onto the upper rung and off again to demonstrate how secure it was.

'Shall I go first, or you?' he asked.

'You lead and I'll follow,' I said.

Halfway down the ladder my hands were sticky and I was holding on much tighter than I needed to. All the same, with his reassuring voice encouraging my every step, I made it to the next level and began to feel a little better. Another ladder came next, followed by a huge, wide ramp that gradually evened out onto a second platform. In this manner we worked steadily downwards, pausing from time to time so that I could get some perspective on our progress, then continuing unhurriedly to the next stage. As we did so I marvelled at how well it had all been worked out. The ladders were fixed firmly in position and the ramps of earth packed hard so that they felt very solid underfoot. Consequently, none of the links in this stairway was daunting enough to make me want to turn back. At one point there was even a wooden bench for resting on, and when we reached it my guide suggested we stopped for a few minutes. Another good idea. So far I'd managed to avoid looking into the canyon itself, but when I finally did I discovered I was able to remain calm and composed. This was actually quite enjoyable! As we sat gazing across the wide expanse, I noticed that several of the people below were staring up at us. Presumably, they must have seen many others coming down this route in the past, and I wondered what they found so interesting about my partner and me.

Most of them, however, were concentrating fully on their task. All along the canyon, huge excavations were under way to make it broader, deeper and longer, the work being carried out by highly-organized groups of men and women. Everywhere there were ramps, ladders and hoists, as well as planks and footpaths connecting the various operations. The area around the encampment was apparently finished, because the earth here had been levelled completely flat. Even so, there was still plenty remaining to be done, and all of a sudden I felt a desire to take part in this tremendous undertaking.

'Shall we go on?' I said.

My neighbour had been sitting in silence, as if contemplating the upturned faces below. Now he rose to his feet, saying, 'Yes, of course', and led the way to the next stage.

Trudging up from the bottom was a straggler, a lone man on the first leg of his journey home. He was moving very slowly, carefully measuring his steps, as he negotiated a ramp, a ladder and then another ramp. He paused at the foot of the next ladder, seemingly unaware that we were waiting above him. My companion leaned over and called, 'Do you want to come up first, John?'

The question had a marked effect on the man below us. He glanced up, saw who'd addressed him, and gave a cry of recognition.

'Michael!' he exclaimed. 'Oh yes, thank you, I will!'

17

So, had I met him at last? Was I being led down this obstacle course by Michael Hawkins himself? The sudden realization that, yes, I most probably was, caused me to sway unsteadily and next moment I felt him seize me by the arm.

'Careful now,' he said. 'The most difficult part's already done.'

'Yes,' I replied, striving to recover my balance. 'I'm just beginning to understand that.'

We remained there, with him gently supporting me, as the other man ascended the ladder and joined us.

'Thank you,' he repeated. 'I'm so glad I've caught you, Michael. I need to speak to you and I thought you were up at the top.'

'Is there something wrong?'

'Well, not wrong as such, and I don't want to be a telltale, but Steve Treacle's down there giving out his orders again.'

Michael Hawkins's grip on my arm slackened and then he let go altogether. At the same instant a troubled look crossed his face.

'Alright, thank you, John,' he said at length. 'You've finished work for the time being have you?'

'Yes,' came the reply. 'But I can come back down if anything needs sorting out.'

'No, no, I don't think that will be necessary, thanks all the same. You go home and take some rest, and return whenever you're ready.'

'Alright, well as long as you're sure?'

'Of course,' he said. 'Everything will be fine.'

As John left us and continued climbing I detected a renewed vigour in his step. This I attributed to the brief exchange he'd had with Michael Hawkins, who watched his progress for a while before breathing a long sigh. It was barely audible, and I wouldn't have heard it had I not been listening to him so closely. On our journey down I'd come to depend on his spoken directions. He had a voice I felt I could trust, and now, when I heard him sigh, I knew there was something amiss.

'Problems?' I asked.

'Nothing that can't be resolved.'

'Steve acting up, is he?'

'By the sound of it, yes,' he said. 'Steve today. Someone else tomorrow.'

He looked saddened, and at that moment I forgot about my own concerns.

'Why don't we continue down?' I suggested. 'They probably won't misbehave if you're around.'

'They're not misbehaving really,' he answered. 'It's just that sometimes they try too hard.'

'Oh, well, whatever,' I said. 'Shall we go?'

I was halfway down the ladder before I remembered I was supposed to be afraid of heights, and by then there was no point in worrying about it. Nevertheless, Michael Hawkins carried on talking me down as if I was still under his care, which in many respects was true. I'd arrived in this canyon as a guest of his, and I had to bear in mind that I was very much an outsider. Best to stay close to him, I thought, at least for the time being.

When we finally got to the bottom, it was like entering a whole new world! The first thing I observed was that the climate was milder here than high up on the harsh and windy plain. The desultory flapping of the tarpaulins indicated a gentle breeze, rather than a howling gale, and I could easily imagine the place bathed in summer sunlight. Stretching away in all directions were the great earthworks, swarming with hordes of people all bent on a common purpose. Some of them paused and stared across at us as we passed by, just as they had done during our descent. Michael Hawkins was obviously highly revered in these parts, and as we neared the camp I recalled the impression of him that I'd built up over the past year. It was of a man who could do no wrong, who accomplished great things, and whose whole existence was perfect. These qualities had won him many friends, among them Simon, Steve and Philip. They told me he lived in a better part of the plain than I did. They spread stories about how he'd built a house of tin and then rejected it, leaving an empty shell for me to move into. Everything I heard about him told of his superiority: even his ideas were thought to be more interesting than mine. They abandoned me so that they could go to him, and in this way they'd made me jealous. I now realized that it was envy, not curiosity, that had brought me to see the canyon. It was envy, too, that had made me judge him before we'd even met, and now I felt more than a little ashamed.

*   *   *

'Looks as though supper's almost ready,' he said.

Ahead of us a number of long tables had been set up, around which people were gathering for some food and drink. It seemed like a very sociable affair. We walked another few paces, and then Michael Hawkins suddenly stopped and gazed across to his right. He was examining a level area of land where the work appeared to be more or less finished, but I couldn't really tell what had caught his attention. Then I noticed four wooden pegs. They'd been hammered into the ground to mark a rectangle, roughly the size of a house. A few yards beyond them were another four, laid out in exactly the same manner. He stood for several seconds regarding these pegs in deep thought, and then, without saying a word, he turned and continued towards the camp. Our arrival didn't cause too much of a stir, so when a place was set aside for us at one of the tables I assumed we would be left to eat in peace. No sooner had we sat down, though, than we began to be approached by people with requests. The first was from a man who asked if Michael could spare an hour to view the particular part of the canyon he and his friends were working in.

'We've managed to overcome that little setback,' he explained. 'Following the advice you gave us.'

'That's good,' replied Michael.

'And now we'd like you to see the results.'

'Yes, well, certainly I'll come. Thank you.'

'When do you think that will be?'

'As soon as possible.'

'Tomorrow?'

'Maybe not tomorrow, but very soon, I promise you that.'

The man looked delighted with this news, and said he hoped even greater things would follow such a visit.

Shortly afterwards a second man sidled up to the table.

'Excuse me, Michael,' he said, in a quiet voice. 'Could I ask your opinion on something?'

'Of course.'

'Do you agree that it's better for people to complete the task they've started, rather than just moving willy-nilly from one job to another?'

'Yes,' said Michael. 'What you're saying sounds like good practice to me.'

'And that it's not fair leaving others to see things through?'

'Quite right.'

'Well, could you possibly have a word with Nicholas?' asked the man. 'He's gone off without completing his work and started somewhere else.'

'Ah, Nicholas!' answered Michael, with a smile. 'Yes, I remember he came and asked me about that.'

'Oh . . . did he?'

'Yes, you see his closest companion was working on another site, and they wanted to be together.'

'So it was with your approval, was it?'

'It was indeed.'

'Well, I wish he'd told me.'

'That would have helped, yes, but you know now, so everything's alright.'

'Yes . . . er . . . thank you, Michael. Sorry to bother you.'

And so it continued. Throughout our meal, my host was repeatedly being called on to arbitrate and offer advice, to grant favours and give consent to certain propositions. In doing so he showed infinite patience, always managing to settle issues in a manner acceptable to everyone, and to give praise where it was due. All the same, it struck me that this must be putting a great strain upon the man, and

I wondered if they ever gave him time to himself. For it was his time that they demanded the most. Without exception they appeared to like nothing better than to be seen with him, however briefly, and to have his undivided attention.

Special status had been conferred on me as well, although to a much lesser extent. While Michael Hawkins was dealing as best he could with the various requests, I found myself under the perpetual gaze of a few men and several women. I didn't want to make the same mistake as I had with Jane Day, but even so it was pleasant to be on the receiving end of their smiles and glances. Better still was when Alison Hopewell made an appearance. She was walking amongst the tables, evidently looking for someone, so I called out her name. When she saw me she gave a friendly wave, but her eyes continued searching. A moment later they fell on Michael Hawkins, sitting there beside me. Then she came over.

'Hello,' she said to me. 'So you made it down here after all.'

I didn't even get the chance to answer.

'Oh, Michael,' she continued. 'Do you think you could come over to the new diggings?'

'Yes, I can if you like,' he replied. 'Is something the matter?'

'It's Steve.'

That was all she said, but it was enough to cause a slight murmur to pass around the table.

Michael glanced at me.

'Would you like to come along?' he asked.

'Sure,' I said. 'If you think I can be of help.'

When he rose from his seat one or two other people did likewise, as though to provide strength in numbers.

'No, that's alright,' said Michael. 'Just the three of us will go. The rest of you please stay and enjoy your supper.'

They resumed their meal as we left and headed across the canyon to the far side. This was by way of a footpath of raised earth that passed between several deep excavations. In some of these the people were still working. Others lay empty, with tools and equipment carefully stacked together until next required. Ahead of us the ground was a good bit higher, suggesting operations had only recently begun. This, I assumed, was what Alison had referred to as 'the new diggings'. There were planks laid out to allow access from the footpath, but, drawing nearer, I saw that many more planks remained stacked in a pile, around which stood about a dozen men. One of these turned out to be Steve Treacle.

Even from a distance I could see he was involved in an argument with one of the others. This was quite obvious from his stance, which made him look oddly twisted as he leant forward with his shoulders hunched, jabbing one finger at a man at the other side of the pile. Most of the onlookers were watching intently, while one or two made half-hearted attempts to continue their work. Then someone spotted us coming, and everything changed. Steve's posture relaxed visibly, as if he saw vindication approaching. The other man, in the meantime, took a plank from the pile and stood holding it.

If they expected Michael simply to march up to them and settle the dispute they were wrong. Instead, he picked up a shovel from where it leant against an earth bank, and started digging. Everyone watched in silence as gradually he loaded a barrow until it was full.

Then he turned to the man with the plank and said, 'Could I have that please?'

The man obliged and handed it to Michael, who laid it from the point where he stood to the beginning of the footpath.

'But Michael,' said Steve. 'That's a broad plank.'

'So I see,' replied Michael.

'But we need the broad ones for shoring up the works. Only the ordinary ones are used for running the barrows along. That's how it's been done ever since the beginning.'

'I know,' said Michael. 'Yet clearly I need a plank here, and as far as I can see all those beside you are broad ones.'

'Then I'll run and fetch you an ordinary plank!'

'It won't be necessary.'

'But you told me yourself!' Steve protested. 'I'm only doing as you said! The broad ones are best used for shoring up, that's what you've always told me, but these people won't listen! Please tell them I'm right!'

He looked desperate, and it suddenly seemed as though he was wholly dependent on Michael Hawkins's affirmation. I glanced at Alison, standing beside me with her arms folded, and saw that she was regarding the scene intently, as were the other bystanders.

'Of course you're right, Steve,' said Michael at length. 'It's pleasing to know that you follow my advice so closely, and indeed your compliance is beyond question. Nonetheless, I'm sure you'll agree that we should not allow the means to defeat the end. Won't the broad planks suffice on this one occasion?'

A long moment passed, during which all eyes were on Steve.

'I suppose they could,' he answered, a little stiffly. 'But the general rule still applies, does it?'

'If you wish to call it a rule, then yes,' replied Michael. 'It's just a way of doing things, really.'

While they'd been talking, I'd noticed that a second plank was needed to complete the connection to the footpath. The matter now being settled, I went over to the pile, selected a plank, and placed it end-to-end with Michael's. This simple act, witnessed by a dozen people, had consequences I could never have predicted. I meant only to ease Michael's burden a little, yet by moving that plank without asking permission from him, from Steve, or from anyone else, I bestowed authority upon myself.

18

That night, for the first time in my life, I slept beneath a tarpaulin. It was most pleasant. The fabric provided adequate protection in the mild conditions of the canyon, and life under cloth made an interesting change from the rigours of a tin house. There was none of the creaking and groaning to which I'd become accustomed over the years, nor were there shutters and doors to be opened and closed at certain intervals. Instead there were only flaps, which could be lowered for additional privacy, or rolled up to allow the circulation of air. As I said, it made an interesting change, but it was nothing more than that.

I soon gathered from the conversations of those around me, however, that they regarded their stay here as a sort of duty, an unavoidable preface to the day when the city of tin would be rebuilt on this very spot.

As a matter of fact, this was all they ever talked about. As I drifted off to sleep, the last thing I heard was my neighbours discussing their plans for tin walls, tin roofs and tin chimneys. Next morning, when I awoke to pale light filtering through canvas, the same voices were still deep in conversation. Oh, what hopes they had! It seemed they liked nothing more, after three or four days' work, than to return to their homes and dream, safe in the knowledge that for the time being their service was done.

This work, of course, was carried out at Michael Hawkins's behest, and I had to admit that his accomplishments were astounding. Even when I joined one of the squads and took part in operations myself, I just couldn't see how we managed to move so much earth. If one man filled a barrow, and led it off along the planks and footpaths, then by the time he returned his comrades would have filled ten more. These tens soon became hundreds, and so on, until the excavation was complete, and we could move on. Every now and then Michael would pay a visit to see that all was going well, and then they would bombard him with questions such as those I'd heard on the first evening. Quite often, though, he would be away surveying some other part of the canyon, and it was on these occasions that they turned to me instead. Apparently, word had got round about the incident involving the planks, and it was now generally assumed that I could speak for Michael. So it was that my opinion began to be sought on all kinds of matters, from the settlement of disputes over who should be working where, to the correct method for handling a shovel. The majority of enquiries, however, concerned the proposed city, and I soon discovered there was something Michael hadn't told them.

Thanks to him, they now knew how to dig a canyon, deep and wide enough to house as many people as wanted to live there. They had also learned the techniques of building from tin, the ideal lengths for chimneys, and the importance of shutters and doors. But what they still didn't know was when they could move from the old site to the new.

It seemed that whenever they asked Michael, he would evade the question, or answer it in a circuitous way that left them no wiser.

Once I'd been among them for a few days I started to sense that they were becoming impatient over this. After all, they said, hadn't they done as he'd instructed? Hadn't they worked hard every day, only to sleep at night under tarpaulins? When, they wanted to know, could they build their promised city?

These particular queries, I noticed, were never put directly to Michael himself. None of them wished to appear ungrateful for what he'd done for them, and not for one minute would they think of complaining. All the same, it was clear they'd like to know more.

Even Alison Hopewell, who had always struck me as being the most level-headed of people, showed signs of restlessness. It was she who helped me find nightly accommodation under the tarpaulins, and after that we tended to spend a lot of time together. We even worked on the same excavation. Alison wasn't quite as overawed by Michael as the rest of them, and one day, while we were walking back to the camp, she told me she'd been to see him.

'What about?' I enquired.

'I asked him when we could start building the new city, and you know what he said?'

'No.'

'He said, "There's a great step ahead of us". What do you think he meant by that?'

'Not sure, really.'

'He talks in riddles sometimes.'

'Yes.'

Alison glanced at me. 'You don't think he's just playing games with us?'

'No,' I replied. 'Shouldn't think so.'

'Cos if he is I'll . . .' She trailed off. 'What's Simon up to?'

We were now approaching the area where I'd noticed the eight wooden pegs in the ground. Just to one side of them was Simon Painter, busily engaged in measuring out a section of land. He walked about ten paces, stopped, and hammered in a new peg. Then he turned sharp right, marched another few steps, and paused again.

'Come on,' said Alison, veering off the footpath in Simon's direction. I followed, and we joined him just as he finished putting in the next peg.

'Simon, what do you think you're doing?' she asked.

'Oh hello,' he said. 'I'm just marking out the site for my house.'

Anyone who'd been in the canyon more than a day was usually caked with grime. Simon, however, looked comparatively fresh, as though he'd only just arrived. This should have set him at some advantage over Alison, who was tired and work-stained after a day in the excavations. Unfortunately for him, it went the other way. I could tell by his expression that he saw absolutely nothing wrong with hammering pegs into the ground. He was therefore ill-prepared for the onslaught that followed.

'The site for your house?' she repeated.

'Yes,' he said. 'This is the first spot to catch the sun in the morning. It's just perfect.'

'So you've taken it for yourself, have you?'

'Along with Steve and Philip, yes. Those other pegs are for their houses.'

'I can't believe I'm hearing this,' said Alison. 'I mean, what if I'd come and put a lot of pegs in. What then?'

'You'd have had to take them out again,' replied Simon.

'Why?'

'Because we were here before you.'

'What difference does that make?'

'Well—' he began, but that was all he managed.

'Don't you dare!' cried Alison. 'You can't just go grabbing land for yourselves when there are so many of us working! Who do you think you are, exactly?!'

'We're Michael's closest friends.'

I looked at Simon and realized that he believed what he said was true. He really thought that he, Steve and Philip occupied some privileged position. A glance around the canyon told a different story. From all directions came workers heading back to camp, each of whom were convinced they had a special affinity with Michael Hawkins. Several dozen had already left the footpath and wandered over to find out what the fuss was about. Now they stood watching as Simon made his preposterous claim.

'We're all his friends!' announced Alison. 'You and your cronies are just trying to steal a march on the rest of us.'

'No, we're not!' protested Simon. 'We're preparing the ground, that's all.'

This sounded rather lame to me, and I wasn't surprised when it brought a jeer from the onlookers.

'Nonsense,' said a voice behind me. It belonged to Patrick Pybus. I turned and saw him coming forward with six or seven other people in tow. These I recognized as some of the fresh-faced volunteers from the city. They didn't seem quite so friendly now, and all at once Simon's situation appeared less than secure.

'Hello, Patrick,' I said, attempting to lighten matters. 'How are you settling in?'

'How can anyone settle in?' he demanded. 'When none of us is ever told what's happening. Day after day we've been waiting for the word to come, and still we hear nothing. All we get is these so-called friends of Michael telling us what we can and cannot do!'

Everyone now looked at Simon, who had suddenly raised his hand for silence.

'Michael says we should be patient,' he announced.

This provoked another jeer, and I realized that if he kept on coming out with such unwise remarks he was going to be in serious trouble. Quickly, I stepped towards him and removed the hammer and pegs from his grasp. Then, watched by many eyes, I went round the other pegs and pulled them out of the ground. A murmur of approval came from the crowd as I did this, and I hoped it would be enough to get them to disperse. Next instant, however, there was a flurry and someone said, 'Here's Michael.'

It was extraordinary the way they parted to let him through. The confrontation with Simon had caused their number to swell to more than a hundred, yet Michael passed between them with ease, pursued by a question coming as from one voice: 'When shall we build our city of tin?'

Walking behind him were Steve Treacle and Philip Sibling, who looked most put out when the jostling mob surged around them. Only Michael himself was given room to move, and it was with some difficulty that these two managed to keep up. Steve had a bustling manner about him, and I almost expected to hear a shout of 'Make way!' as he followed after Michael. Philip, meanwhile, pushed along as best he could. Both of them were apparently oblivious to the one question being repeated all around them, and seemed only interested in maintaining their role as Michael's guard of honour. It was a role that came to an end when they saw me holding the hammer and pegs.

Without a second thought, they made a rush towards where the rectangles had been. This, of course, separated them from Michael, and within seconds they were lost, powerless to move, in the midst of the seething crowd. For a moment I feared for their safety, but, luckily for them, everyone's attention was on Michael. He, too, had noticed the hammer and pegs in my hand. He approached and took them from me.

'When shall we build our city of tin?!' went up the cry.

Michael held the implements aloft. His audience fell silent.

'The next time we use this hammer and these pegs,' he declared, 'it will be for all your houses!'

A great cheer ensued, and from my place in the crowd I could feel anticipation stirring.

'There's something I've been meaning to tell you for a long while!' he continued. 'But it had to wait until I felt you were ready! Now, at last, the day has come, and the question can be answered! You ask me when shall we build our city of tin, and I say to you: Never!'

During the few moments it took for his words to sink in, most of the people around me just stood there gaping. Then a groan of disappointment such as I had never heard arose and threatened to drown him out.

'Never?!' said Alison. 'What do you mean, never?'

'This is the great step I told you about,' replied Michael. 'We have no more need for tin! Why? Because there's clay here! Now we can make bricks and tiles! We can build proper houses, with foundations, and walls that won't creak and groan at every breath of wind!'

'We don't know how to build from clay,' said Patrick Pybus. 'We only know about tin.'

'You can learn,' Michael answered. 'And as you learn,

you can build. Build a great city of clay in this canyon you've created!'

'But we already have a city of tin!' someone called from the back, to noisy acclaim.

'Abandon it!' he commanded. 'Let it stand as a monument to your folly and your lost aspirations! From this day on, we build only from clay!'

There followed a brief lull, during which one or two individuals near the front repeated what they'd just heard. 'We build only from clay,' they said, as if testing the sound of it for themselves. 'From this day on, we build only from clay.' These words were taken up by a few other people, then more, and then more still, and gradually the doctrine spread. In small groups and in pairs they began to discuss Michael's latest pronouncement. It had been a shock, for they'd assumed they only had to dig a canyon and their city could be founded overnight. Now, it seemed, a further step remained.

As I watched them drift back to the encampment, I realized he had won their obedience yet again. From now on they would build only from clay.

It was an outcome I found most gratifying.

19

In some respects I felt quite sorry for Simon, Steve and Philip. They had, after all, been pioneers in their particular field, and now at a stroke it was being snatched away from them. To live in a house of tin had ceased to be the great ideal. As a result, their knowledge of the subject offered no advantage. Previously they'd managed to persuade themselves that it might win them favour with Michael, but the episode with the pegs had shown them otherwise. He'd moved forward, and their only hope was to follow his lead and take their place in the city of clay.

To their credit, they seemed quickly to have grasped this, and they buckled down to the new regime within a couple of days. It was clear, though, that some of their habits weren't going to change. At any particular time, for example, Steve could still be seen marching up to some work party or other and dishing out all sorts of orders. The difference now was that no one took the slightest bit of notice, as word of his powerlessness went before him. Undeterred, he managed to put himself in charge of the hoists, which everyone agreed was a good channel for his energy. The fact that nobody else wanted the job didn't appear to bother him. Philip, of course, was always at hand to lend assistance, and the two of them spent many an hour maintaining an apparatus that actually required no attention.

Simon, meanwhile, had set himself the task of designing a flag to fly above his new house. His former optimism had returned apace, and he was convinced he would be amongst the first residents of the completed city. Nightly, he went round the encampment trying to muster support for his proposition that every dwelling should eventually have its own flag. Like Steve and Philip, however, he was no longer taken seriously.

For my part, I found myself spending more and more time in the company of women, though maybe I should add that relations between us never went beyond ordinary friendship, since it was impossible to obtain sufficient privacy under those tarpaulins even if the flaps were rolled down. Indeed, the place was beginning to get quite crowded. Fresh recruits were continuing to arrive in the canyon, and they, too, had to be accommodated. Sometimes I looked around and wondered where they were all going to live, but on each occasion I had to admit that the operation was fully under control. Michael appeared to be going from strength to strength. The dual supply of clay and manpower meant he had all the resources he needed, and as the canyon expanded, so did his enthusiasm for the work. Even Alison Hopewell managed to get swept along in it. Her aloofness had faded and she was now amongst the first to rise in the morning, frequently offering to go and assist him when he surveyed some new terrain. They would come back hours later, full of the joys of spring.

*   *   *

Yet there was one who doubted him. Jane Day had been Michael's most zealous follower, and I thought that she of all people would fall straight into line and accept the changes without demur. Instead, when she heard that the city of tin was to be forsaken, she raised a voice of protest. This amounted to little more than a whinge: a petty complaint that bore no substance. Nevertheless, it was enough to sow the seed. Her misgivings emerged one day when a group of us, including Jane and Sarah, were working on the clay beds, preparing for the production of bricks and tiles. There were numerous kilns to be constructed before we could even think of building the city itself, and most people recognized that the whole process was going to be a slow one. Jane, however, seemed rapidly to be losing interest. As a consequence, she began to seek faults in the man whose idea it had been.

'I suppose Michael will be living apart from the rest of us,' she said. 'When this new city is finished.'

'It's possible,' I replied. 'The tin house that stands alone is his, I presume?'

'Yes,' said Jane. 'Meanwhile, the rest of us all get packed together. I expect he'll have one half of the canyon, and we'll have to share the remainder.'

'Well, I think Michael deserves some space to himself,' remarked one of the other women. 'After all he's done for us.'

'And what's that exactly?'

The abruptness of Jane's question caused those nearby to stop work and look round. It had clearly caught the woman unprepared, for she hesitated a moment without making any reply. This lapse provided Jane with a further opening.

'I'll tell you what he's done,' she said. 'He's played a trick on us.'

'Oh Jane!' exclaimed Sarah, 'How can you say that when he's building a great new city, entirely from clay?'

'Cos I want to live in a house of tin!' cried Jane at the top of her voice. 'That's why I came here in the first place!'

'So did we all,' said Sarah, 'But now Michael's asked us to take a further step.'

This caused Jane to laugh aloud. 'And then what after that? Eh? What will the next step be then? Another promise? Something else to keep us working like slaves? If you want my opinion he's led us all a merry dance and we've fallen for it! At this rate we'll be stuck here waiting forever!'

Sarah gazed at her dumbfounded, and next moment Jane had gone stalking off towards the footpath. The whole party watched in silence as she made her way across the canyon towards the ladders, and then began climbing upwards.

'Are you alright?' someone asked Sarah, who looked a little shaken.

'Just about,' she replied, staring at Jane's diminishing figure. 'I don't know what's come over her lately.'

'Well, she has got a point hasn't she?'

This last comment came from a man I'd met once before, at Simon Painter's house. On that occasion he'd directed us all to listen to the wind under the eaves, as though it was some great and original discovery he'd just made. For this reason I didn't much care for him. Now, it seemed, he was taking Jane's side of the argument.

'What point's that then?' I enquired. 'Just out of interest.'

'You should know,' he said. 'You're supposed to be the great exponent of tin.'

'Maybe I am, but I've still no idea what you're talking about.'

'It's simple,' he replied. 'Jane wants to live in a tin house, that's all. She's not interested in these so-called extra steps.'

'And you agree with her, do you?'

'To an extent, yes.'

'But in the long run we'll be better off with clay, surely,' said Sarah.

'Well, if you wish to believe that it's up to you,' he answered. 'To tell the truth I've had enough.'

As the debate continued, other members of the party began to join in, all offering different points of view. It soon transpired that some among them were less than convinced about the possibilities Michael had to offer. They were still prepared to give it a go, they said, but this building from clay looked like it was a hard slog. How much easier it would be to live in a city of tin.

I decided to keep my own counsel on the matter, and was about to resume work when I noticed a woman descending the ladder that Jane had just gone up. Her movements were very familiar, so I continued watching until she arrived at the bottom, where she stood glancing around as if trying to get her bearings. Obviously a new-comer, I concluded, but next second I realized it was Mary Petrie!

Downing tools I set off to meet her, pondering what could have brought her all this way. Then suddenly it struck me that something must have happened to the house! On the verge of panic I broke into a run, tearing along planks and footpaths to the other side of the canyon. Mary Petrie saw me coming and waited.

'You're as bad as that woman on the ladder,' she said,

as I dashed up. 'She nearly knocked me off, she was in such a hurry.'

'Is anything wrong?' I asked, after an appropriate embrace.

'I was going to ask you that,' she replied.

'Why?'

'Because you didn't come back, of course!'

'Oh, right,' I said. 'Well, I'll tell you the reason.'

I then gave her the full story of my arrival, of all the people I'd met, and how I'd stayed a while to help with the canyon. This took about ten minutes, and when I'd finished Mary Petrie said, 'Don't bother asking how I've been, will you?'

'How have you been?' I asked.

'I'm OK,' she replied. 'And you'll be pleased to know that your precious house is still standing.'

'It should be,' I said. 'Apparently Michael built it.'

'Oh yes, the great Michael Hawkins! I can't wait to make his acquaintance.'

'Michael's alright when you get to know him,' I remarked. 'He's got big plans for this place.'

'So I gather,' she said. 'It's all they talk about in the tin city.'

'Oh, you've been there, have you? What did you think?'

'Quite sweet really, although I couldn't live there.'

'Why not?'

'Cos they talk such nonsense all the time. Really, I thought you were a bit obsessive, but at least you've got your head screwed on properly. This lot babble on and on about tin houses and clay houses, and it's obvious they don't know what they're talking about.'

'Well, that's as may be,' I replied. 'But you have to watch what you say round here: they're a bit touchy on the subject.'

'I don't care,' said Mary Petrie. 'I've told you before, it's not where you live that counts but who you live with.'

'I know, I know, but just while we're here . . . ?'

'Well, how long's that going to be?'

'I'm not sure,' I said. 'It depends.'

Such an answer, needless to say, was totally unsatisfactory, and Mary Petrie seemed on the verge of telling me so when our conversation was interrupted. It was the time of day when volunteers who'd done their three or four days' service left the canyon and were replaced by fresh recruits from the city. As a result, the area around the foot of the ladder became fairly busy for a while, and we were obliged to move out of the way. We watched as the various squads passed by and began their ascent. These included the group I'd recently been working with on the clay beds.

'They're having a few days' rest,' I explained.

'What about you?' asked Mary Petrie. 'Aren't you going up as well?'

'No, I don't usually bother,' I said. 'I'd much rather stay down here under the tarpaulins.'

This wasn't entirely true, of course, as my preferred dwelling would always be one of tin. The real problem was that I felt unable to tackle the climb again without Michael being present, and he hadn't left the canyon for some time now. As a result, neither had I. Every time the others trooped home for a break I'd made some excuse about staying behind to help out, and they'd believed me because of my well-known independent ways. A little later the next batch would arrive, noisily enthusiastic as they came down the ramps and ladders, and I would be amongst the first to greet them.

As it turned out, there was only a trickle of people this evening. The few who descended and headed for the encampment were nowhere near enough to replace those who'd just left, and vaguely I wondered what had happened to the rest.

'Come on,' I said. 'It's time to have something to eat.'

I was aware that the camp would not be Mary Petrie's kind of place at all, so rather than head there directly I took her on a brief tour first. We followed a meandering route along the various planks and footpaths as I showed her the excavations where I'd been involved, and then we called on Steve and Philip. They were carrying out some maintenance on one of the hoists. The moment Steve saw Mary Petrie he stopped work and started giving her a full technical explanation of how it operated. I could tell she wasn't at all interested in the subject, and thought she showed remarkable forbearance in listening politely until he'd finished. After asking one or two questions in the manner of a visiting dignitary, she then began slowly to move away, leaving Steve stranded in mid-sentence as he rambled on about ropes and pulleys.

He turned to me with a blank expression.

'Been busy here?' I enquired.

'Not really,' he said. 'People only dig at half-speed when Michael's not around.'

'Where is he today then?'

'Surveying the far end of the canyon.'

'With Alison Hopewell?'

'Yes.'

'That makes a change. Er . . . look, I'd better go and catch up with Mary. Otherwise I'll risk incurring her wrath: you know what she can be like.'

'I do indeed,' replied Steve. 'But all the same it's nice to see her again.'

'Suppose it is, yes.'

Mary Petrie had meanwhile wandered along to the clay beds, where she stood gazing vaguely at the work in progress.

'By the way,' she said, when I joined her. 'I met another of your friends up in the city.'

'Who was that?'

'Patrick Pybus.'

'Oh, him,' I said. 'He's not a friend really: he just tagged on to me, that's all.'

'Well, he speaks very highly of you.'

'Does he?'

'Oh yes,' she said. 'You seem to be quite popular.'

'That's because I know all about tin houses,' I pointed out. 'As soon as they've started building from clay they'll forget I exist.'

While we were there I took the opportunity to show her the site for the kilns. It was evident she was beginning to tire, however, so I next steered her towards the encampment, where food was about to be served. As usual, a place was set aside for me at one of the tables, and I think this impressed Mary Petrie. Nonetheless, I was concerned that she might object to sleeping under the tarpaulins. If she did, I had no idea how I would resolve the matter.

During supper I noticed that quite a lot of the conversation was about Jane Day and her outburst during the afternoon. I would have expected her opinions to be condemned out of hand, at least publicly, so I was surprised to hear a number of sympathetic comments, even from those who fully accepted that clay was better than tin.

The debate drew swiftly to a close when Michael Hawkins returned. He was accompanied by Alison, who looked somewhat drained and retired immediately to bed. I then took the opportunity to introduce Mary Petrie to Michael.

He was charm itself, welcoming her warmly and disclosing that the plans for the first houses were now ready.

'We'll start digging the foundations tomorrow,' he announced, glancing at me. 'How are the kilns coming along?'

'Not too bad,' I said. 'Although we're a bit short-handed.'

A troubled look crossed Michael's face, and he cast his eyes around the tables.

'Yes, you're right,' he agreed. 'Where is everybody?'

'Up in the city of tin, I suppose.'

'Well, could you do me a favour and count how many we've got down here?'

'Yes,' I said. 'Sure.'

Michael often asked me to carry out small but important tasks of this nature, so I wasn't at all surprised by the request. As soon as I'd finished supper I went round the tables counting up, and then made a circuit of the outlying excavations to see if anyone was working late. It turned out that nobody was, so the total amount of people available to work numbered less than eighty. This was in stark contrast to the hundreds that usually flocked into the canyon, and when I returned to Michael I felt like I was the bearer of bad news.

'Not to worry,' he said, apparently unperturbed. 'We'll just have to have a recruitment drive, that's all.'

During my absence he and Mary Petrie seemed to have been getting on very well together. She'd already agreed to accompany him on a surveying trip the following day, and had gone to bed early in preparation.

'I've organized a place for her under the tarpaulins,' he said. 'She should be nice and snug there.'

20

The first thing I discovered on awaking next morning was that more workers had slipped away during the night. Why they should depart in such an underhand manner was beyond me, as Michael had always been very frank and open with them. No one had been coerced into coming to this canyon, or detained against their wishes, yet by the time I arose another three dozen had sneaked off as if making an escape! Wandering over for some breakfast I saw Simon, Steve and Philip sitting at a table deep in discussion, so I went and joined them. For a few moments they failed to acknowledge me, though I knew they'd seen my approach. Then abruptly Simon turned to me and said, 'You know about the latest mutterings, do you?'

'No,' I replied. 'Why, what have you heard?'

'People are saying that Jane Day was expelled from the canyon for her outspokenness.'

'Expelled?'

'Driven into exile by Michael himself.'

'But that's ridiculous!' I said. 'She went of her own accord!'

'We're simply telling you what people are saying,' murmured Philip. 'To put you in the picture.'

'Well, I hope you three have been setting them straight with a few facts!' I snapped.

'Nothing to do with us,' said Steve.

He uttered this with an air of sulkiness that I'd have thought was below him. Meanwhile, Simon and Philip gazed at me in resignation.

'So are you all just going to sit and wash your hands of the whole affair?' I asked.

'What more can we do?' answered Simon with a shrug. 'We've tried, but no one listens to us any more.'

*   *   *

For the rest of the day a sort of hiatus descended on the encampment. None of those who remained were inclined to do any work, and instead they passed the time gathered together in small groups, kicking their heels and chatting. I spent a while ambling around the clay beds, repositioning planks and so forth, but soon I, too, lost momentum.

The buckets on the hoist swung empty and unused as Steve and the others continued their conversation around the table. From a distance I noticed Alison Hopewell emerge from beneath the tarpaulins and approach them. She had a rather agitated manner, I thought, and was pacing around the table gesticulating with her hands. Something had clearly upset her, so I began walking over to see what was wrong, but suddenly she went marching away along one of the footpaths. I followed for a few hundred yards, unable to catch up, and finally decided that she most likely wanted to be left alone. For this reason I turned back.

At some point in the afternoon it occurred to me that Michael would most probably have left too early to be aware of the further decrease in numbers. I knew that his presence alone could reverse the situation, and with this in mind I set off to find him and Mary Petrie. I met them a little later, strolling side by side in the direction of the camp, but obviously in no hurry to arrive there. When they saw me coming they quickened their pace.

'What is it?' asked Michael.

'Well I think you should get back as soon as you can,' I replied. 'There's hardly anyone left.'

This was borne out when we drew near and saw the tarpaulins flapping unattended in the early evening breeze. The tables were deserted, as were the nearby walkways. It appeared that even Simon, Steve and Philip had gone, and when we glanced towards the ladders we saw the last of the defectors receding over the top. Michael halted and stood gazing round at the work he'd begun, but which now seemed doomed to failure. The whole place lay silent and desolate beneath the canyon walls that were to have sheltered his people. Even the clay beds, opened so very recently, were fast becoming cracked and dry. The prospects for building a great new city looked slim indeed.

All of a sudden Michael turned to us and clapped his hands together. 'Very well!' he declared. 'If they won't come to me, I'll just have to go to them!'

Next instant he was striding across the canyon floor towards the ascent route, with Mary Petrie following close behind. She'd said little since returning, and instead spent most of the time listening intently to what Michael had to say. In her eyes was a look I'd never seen before.

I, too, felt a desire to accompany Michael, not least because without him I couldn't face the ladders. He was already halfway up the first one when I arrived at the bottom, so I seized the rungs and climbed blindly after him. There were no reassuring words to help me on this journey, as there had been coming down, so I had little choice but to do exactly as he did, putting my hands and feet where he put his, and resting when he rested. Mary Petrie did likewise, and the three of us climbed steadily up the ladders and ramps before finally emerging onto the plain. At once I felt on my face the harsh wind that until a few weeks ago had been so familiar, but which I'd gradually forgotten in the benign climate below. As my companions went ahead, I paused a while and took a last look into the canyon, certain now that I would not be going back. Then I turned and set off in pursuit of the others.

I wasn't sure whether Michael intended to go direct to the tin city, or call first at his own house, which as I said before was set some distance apart. Perhaps, I thought, he would go there to rest and prepare himself, or maybe rehearse a speech, prior to approaching his absent followers. If so I'd get the chance to see at first hand the finest tin house of them all: the one chosen by the man himself. This was something I'd wanted to do ever since I'd first laid eyes on the place, but as it turned out I never even got near to it. While I'd been walking I had gradually become aware of much activity outside the city walls, and by the time I caught up with Michael it was apparent that a vast throng had gathered there.

'Looks like they're having some kind of meeting,' I said. 'What do you think that's about?'

'Well, we'll soon know,' he replied. 'They've seen us coming.'

Even as he spoke we heard a shout, and next moment some members of the crowd began to surge towards us. Others, however, continued milling around where they were, and seemed to waver before eventually following the general flow. The result was a ragged procession of people coming towards us, a procession whose purpose appeared far from certain.

'Be careful, won't you?' urged Mary Petrie, as Michael went forward to meet the vanguard.

'It'll be alright,' he said. 'They just need a few words of guidance, that's all.'

I wasn't so sure. From where I stood this leading mob looked to be getting enough guidance already. At its forefront strode Patrick Pybus, with Jane, Sarah and their band of associates all close at hand, talking in loud voices and offering raucous encouragement to one another. Ignoring the hesitancy of those further back, they forged quickly ahead as if having taken matters into their own hands. This was confirmed when Patrick marched up and presented himself as spokesman, clasping Michael in a brotherly embrace and making a great show of welcoming him.

Then he said, 'We're glad you're here because we've just arrived at an important decision. All it needs is your approval.'

'I see,' replied Michael. 'Well then. Tell me what it is you've decided.'

'We think we should have the freedom to choose between tin or clay.'

Patrick made his announcement in a steady tone which was neither demand nor request. Instead, he talked as though he was stating a fact, uncompromising and simple, the sanctioning of which would be a mere formality. He seemed quite pleased, nonetheless, when Michael said, 'Yes, of course you're free to choose.'

'You've no objection then?' asked Patrick. 'If we stick to tin?'

'None at all,' came the reply. 'If you wish to stay here on this plain it's entirely up to you.'

Patrick's face fell. 'Oh no,' he said. 'You misunderstand me. We want to move into the canyon.'

'But that's not possible,' said Michael.

'Why?'

'Because I won't allow it.'

During this brief conversation numerous other people had come along and begun gradually to surround us, while still more were closing in from behind. Judging by their expressions they didn't all share the opinion of Patrick and his accomplices. Some clearly disagreed: others remained undecided. Soon these various factions were joined by the many who had caught nothing of what was being said, and who were now straining hard to listen, jostling one another for a better place. On their faces were looks of sheer bewilderment. They crowded together in a huge seething mass, confused and fearful of the momentous choice that awaited them.

'You won't allow it?' somebody asked in a mocking tone. 'You won't allow tin houses?'

It was the voice of Jane Day, and when I glanced in her direction I knew at once that she was enjoying every second of this encounter. She stood in the thick of the mob, sneering with glee as she awaited Michael's response. For my part, I was alarmed by his high-handed manner. Over the past weeks I'd been most impressed with the subtle way in which he'd dealt with his followers, always allowing room for dissent and never speaking down to them. Now

I realized that even Michael had his limitations. These circumstances clearly demanded the utmost diplomacy, yet suddenly he appeared to be digging his heels in. It was almost as if he was deliberately placing himself in a predicament, and Jane Day was quick to recognize the fact.

'Come on!' she demanded. 'Give us an answer!'

'You already know the answer,' replied Michael. 'You cannot come into my canyon unless you build from clay.'

'Cannot?' said Jane, raising her voice. 'Cannot?!'

She jabbed a finger into Michael's chest. He yielded a little. Some members of the crowd took this to be a sign of weakness and began jeering. Thus encouraged, Jane prodded him again. 'Cannot?!' she bayed, as he stepped back and lost his balance. Hands stretched out to support him, but in the same instant others grabbed hold and began pulling him towards them. 'Seize him!' they yelled. 'He's ours!' The mob pressed in and Michael was roughly bundled from one group to the next in a desperate struggle for possession. Meanwhile Jane capered wildly amongst them issuing frenzied commands. 'Tear him apart!' she screeched. 'Pull him to pieces!' Next thing they had their captive by the arms and legs and were heaving him in all four directions. Mary Petrie swung round at me, her eyes blazing. 'Do something!' she cried. 'You're the only one they'll listen to!'

A distant glimmer caught my eye.

'His house!' I bellowed. 'Tear his house to pieces instead!'

'His house!' echoed Mary Petrie in desperation. 'His house, his house!'

At the fringe of the crowd I could see Simon, Steve and Philip, trying in vain to get through. Their intention was unclear, but when they heard my shout they immediately veered away and began racing towards the lone tin structure. Several people peeled off after them, then more still, enabling me to get closer to those holding onto Michael.

'Not him, his house!' I roared, over and over, until at last they heard me, loosening their grip one by one and dashing away to where the demolition had already started. At last there remained only Jane Day. With a shriek she dodged round me and attempted to batter Michael, now lying motionless on the ground. Mary Petrie saw her off in a trice, emitting a fierce howl that scared the wits out of her, and chasing her halfway to the city before turning back.

A groan from Michael told me he was still intact, so I helped him to his feet and watched as he stumbled towards the open plain. From the direction of his house of tin there came a great clamour. The destruction was now complete and each person grabbed whatever he could. As I watched, however, it quickly became clear that there weren't enough pieces to go round, and soon arguments and fights began breaking out amongst the plunderers. Then all at once the entire horde made a rush towards the city, bent on a course of action I couldn't quite make out. Only when they set upon their own houses did I understand. They swarmed around the walls and over the roofs, pulling them apart, and throwing them down into haphazard stacks. Off came the shutters and the doors, the chimneys and the drain-pipes, all the different sizes mixed up together. Squads of people gathered up the assorted pieces and began carrying them towards the canyon, leaving them at the brink before returning for more.

I remained at the centre of all this chaos feeling quite uninvolved. I knew now that I had only to wait. After a while Mary Petrie joined me and asked what had happened to Michael. I pointed to a remote figure.

'I must go and comfort him,' she said.

*　　*　　*

Darkness was beginning to fall, yet still the dwindling city continued to be dismantled, piled up and carried away. No one seemed to have stopped to think how they were going to put it all together again. Instead they ordered each other around, and squabbled over the gleaming components as night descended and the moon appeared. Eventually, there was nothing whole to be seen: all that remained of the city was a collection of tin, teetering at the edge of the canyon. I could hear the hoists being operated as attempts were made to lower the various sections. More often, though, I heard arguments about how it should be done. Some people tried carrying pieces down the ladders and ramps, but there were frequent accidents, or they became lost in the deepening gloom. Others stole from their former companions. There were shouts, and clangs, and still more shouts. And in the midst of it all I could hear the plaintive voice of a woman, calling out, 'Where is he?! Where has he gone?!'

*　　*　　*

Around midnight, while I sat observing the mayhem, I was approached by a party of three men. They were led by Patrick Pybus.

'We don't know what to do,' he said. 'Our city is in ruins and we need guidance.'

'Well, how do you expect me to give you the answer?' I replied, 'if you wouldn't even listen to Michael?'

'He asked too much of us,' said Patrick. 'We just wanted a better place to live, that was all.'

'Then there's only one thing you can do, and if I tell you, you won't like it.'

'Tell us anyway,' said another man. 'Please.'

'Only if you promise to obey me.'

'We will!' exclaimed Patrick. 'Only tell us!'

'Very well.'

I rose to my feet and stood for a long time regarding their upturned faces. Then I gave my judgement.

'You must cast your tin over the precipice!' I said. 'And go back to where you came from!'

21

I live in a house built entirely from tin, with four tin walls, a roof of tin, a chimney and door. Entirely from tin.

My house has no windows because there's nothing to see. Oh, there are shutters that can be opened to let the light in when required, but mostly they remain closed against the weather. It stands in a wild place, my house, high up on the plain. At night it creaks and groans as the wind hammers it for hour after hour, seeking a gap to get inside. I used to worry that in such harsh conditions it might one day fall apart. Now, though, I'm certain the structure is quite sound. The man who built it made sure of that.

I've heard he intends eventually to return and begin his work again. If he does, of course, he will be most welcome as his knowledge is second to none, but so far there's been no sign of him.

From time to time people come wandering onto this plain in search of a better place to be. Some of them say they want to live as I do, protected from the elements by a layer of corrugated metal and nothing more. If they ask me for guidance, I tell them they can find comfort here as long as they don't expect too much. Some stay: others move on.

This house of mine has served me well. Though only built from tin, it held together while kingdoms were being swept away. It is both my refuge and my fortress. Let it be your temple.